A LEGION OF BANE AND EMBERS

A KNIGHTS OF CINDERVAIL NOVEL
BOOK ONE

KL HILL

Cover design by The Red Fox Creative

Interior design and formatting by Sidebar Media, LLC

Editing by Khyla Schmidt, Khyla's Bookshelf

Internal art by Kristen Moreno

First Edition Publication Date: October 17, 2025

Printed in the United States of America

ALSO BY KJ HILL

Masquerave

Coded in Control

Chained to Control

—

Dark Noel

Mistletoe & Naughty

—

Novellas

Spinning Out of Control

Up From Below

AUTHOR'S NOTE

Hello, Little Hillion,

A Legion of Bane and Embers is the first book in the *Knights of Cindervail* series and contains mature, graphic content.

This novel includes sexually explicit scenes, dark themes, and intense emotional and physical elements, violence, and explicit sexual content. It is not suitable for all audiences and is recommended for readers 18+.

Reader discretion is strongly advised.

While I prefer you to go into the story blind, a full list of detailed trigger warnings is available on **www.klhillauthor.com**.

For the full experience, it is recommended that you read the series in order.

xoxo,

    KL Hill

For all the suckers and vampire fuckers.

I

ATLAS

THE RAZOR GLIDES OVER MY CHIN, THE BLADE SNAGGING MY SKIN, tearing it open. *"Fuck,"* I murmur, pressing my fingers to the hard line of my jaw. Pulling them away, their smeared crimson, the bright red drop of blood being lured down my finger by gravity, reaching the deep lines of my palm, following them as if reading my future.

I stiffen as the bathroom door creaks open, followed by a small gust of air and the feeling of someone, or something, behind me. I step closer to the sink and rip the towel from the ring on the wall, pressing it to my face, trying to keep the blood from attracting the monster at my back.

"Just one little lick. I promise not to bite...this time." The voice in my ear is a whisper so soft the wind would carry it away for anyone else, but for me, it burrows in like an earworm, nestling inside until it's all I hear as it eats away at my sanity day after day.

A parasite.

Emilian.

I jerk away, seeing the sharp-toothed monster's reflection in the mirror as he steps out from behind me, his crimson, vampiric eyes flashing. "You know the fucking rules," I bite out through gritted teeth, applying even more pressure to my face. I learned early on that much of the lore we'd been taught about vampires is wildly false.

It was a huge surprise the first time I saw Emilian's reflection in the mirror, or when he drank an entire Bloody Mary loaded with garlic and had no reaction—except for the laugh that escaped as my jaw dropped, proving that not everything written in the tomes is fact.

He quietly groans as he inches closer to me, his pale skin getting lost in the sea of white marble around us. He takes a deep inhale as the blood seeps from my cut, soaking into the towel, the bright red spreading like a disease. I glance at him in the mirror, looking at my mussed brown hair that hangs over the tanned skin of my forehead, careful not to get lost and drown in his depthless eyes as he cages me in, pressing his hardening cock against my backside. "You never let me have any fun with you, Atlas." His voice is low, the sound curling around me, trying to break my defenses—slip through the cracks.

I reach behind me with my free hand and grip the O-ring on the collar that he wears, yanking him to me and forcing him to look at me through the mirror. His crimson eyes flare as he takes an even deeper breath through his nose, inhaling the scent of my blood. His long, sleek black hair falls over half his face, making him look even more menacing. He flashes his teeth, his sharp fangs on full display as he runs his tongue over them, showing them off from behind the cage of his muzzle like a rabid dog— the cool metal that contains his sharp bite gleaming in the bright lights as it brushes against my cheek.

Narrowing my eyes, I pull my finger from the ring and turn, shoving him away. "Keep your filthy hands to yourself, *vermin*. You know the rules." I hold the towel out, pressing it against his muzzle as he takes a deep, growling breath. He reaches for it with a leather-gloved hand, but I pull it back, keeping it just out of reach.

Taunting him.

I bring the towel behind my back, drop it into the deep basin of the sink, and, without looking, grip the faucet handle and turn the water on full blast. He gasps as my blood dilutes in the water and disappears down the drain. He flashes his teeth with disdain, but is no more threatening than a pet on the other side of their chain-linked fence.

"Like I said, you know the fucking rules." I reach behind me and cut the water, the bathroom falling silent except for the rhythmic drip as it hits the soaked towel. "Now, leave me alone and go lock yourself away for the night."

He tries to dazzle me with his vampiric charm as he takes a small step forward, but I'm long immune to it. "I can't do it without your assistance, *sire*." He holds up his wrists, flashing the restraints that have become a permanent fixture.

Scrubbing my hand over my face, trying to keep my expression in check, I wince as I rake my calloused palm over the fresh wound. The smirk on Emilian's face grows into a toothy, monstrous grin as he catches sight of the blood that's smeared across my palm.

Pulling a chain out from my pocket, I run it through my hand, coating it in the fresh blood, before clipping it through the ring at his throat and leashing him. I pull him to me, the metal bars over his face pressing against my nose. He flicks out his tongue, trying for a taste, but the muzzle is long enough to keep me, and everyone else, just out of reach of his infernal mouth.

As a fledgling who was left to his own devices, roaming the city, and looking for his next meal, this was the only way to keep him in control and out of trouble—trouble that could lead to both of our deaths if he's left unchecked.

He's dressed in fighting leathers, with a muzzle connected to his collar at the back of his head. Another leather strap runs down his back, attaching to a leather harness that wraps across his chest and loops around his waist, ensuring that, with enough buckles and enchantments, he can never remove it himself.

Only *I* can.

He holds out his wrists, pressing the cuffs that already adorn them together, his claws threatening to tear through his leather gloves. With my free hand, I clip them together. He lets his arms fall, hanging over the other clip attached to the belt around his waist. I secure him, tugging the metal to ensure he can't break free.

Lowering myself in front of him, I pull another chain out of my pocket, linking the cuffs on his ankles together. He chuckles, and I look up, my eyes passing over the bulge growing in his pants. I narrow my eyes, not even bothering to ask what's so fucking funny as I get back on my feet. "Let's go, you fucking parasite." The words are a growl, rumbling between us, but he smiles as if I confessed my undying love for him.

Motherfucker.

Yanking the chain, I hold a firm grip as I walk out of the bathroom with Emilian in tow. The large townhouse is dimly lit, giving it a Gothic appearance that any historian would envy. The stories of the past press against the walls, begging to be released. It's not my style with its antique details and drafty corners, but when you're left a 5,000 square foot townhouse in a borough of Cindervail, you grab the keys while you can and keep it locked up tight.

We pass by several rooms, including the library study on the main floor with its original wooden details and architecture. The large kitchen, which I remodeled almost immediately, stands out from the rest of the house with its glossy black cabinets and stark white marble countertops and backsplash—the few sconces I choose to keep lit flicker dimly, causing shadows to dance across the walls. The chains between Emilian's legs drag along the floor, with the metal grinding against the hardwood, only quieting as we pass over the antique runners that line the long hall.

I pull open the metal-reinforced wooden door and flick on the lights, casting a dim glow into the basement. I lead him down the stairs, the chains clinking with every step as I bring him back to his dwelling. Stepping off the last step, my shoes tap on the concrete floor, followed by his as he lands at my heels. Pulling the single key from my pocket, I unlock the cell door. The bars span across the space and are securely bolted to the cinderblock walls on each side.

The door creaks open, and I step aside, letting Emilian through first. "Such a gentleman," he croons, his voice wrapping around me, attempting to hook its claws into my skin and pull me under his spell.

My skin heats as he brushes past me, lightly clipping his shoulder with mine. He leads me to the back wall, where a large, reinforced chain is bolted next to his bed. I clip it to the end, snapping the padlock shut around the chain and the O-ring on his collar. I tug it, pulling his face closer to mine. The metal of his muzzle brushes against my lips, and his tongue darts out once more, trying for another taste—one that I promised not to give him again.

I want to shove him back, but my arm is frozen, keeping him in my clutches as I breathe in his musky, intoxicating scent. My head spins as I pull the small wooden stake from where it's holstered at my side. I press the tip against his chest to remind him who his fucking *sire* is, and that even though I didn't change him, he's still mine to deal with. He not only haunts these halls, but my dreams. His crimson eyes follow me, drawing me into the dark.

We stand in heavy silence, his inhale matching my exhale, as if he's drawing the air from my lungs. I blink and pull myself back to reality as his allure fades and my vision clears. I unhook his leash and shove him back. He stumbles slightly, yet he still appears graceful even as he hits the back wall and lets out a quiet breath.

A dark chuckle filters through the bars of his muzzle. "Always so *tempted*," he muses, his eyes flashing as a smile pulls on the corners of his mouth, exposing his fangs. "Always so *curious*."

"Shut the hell up," I growl through clenched teeth. I keep my gaze fixed on him as I back out of his cell, slamming the door shut and snapping the lock in place. I give it a shake, ensuring that the monster can't escape, before turning on my heel and heading up the stairs—as far away from him as I can get while under the same roof.

"Until tomorrow, Atlas." His voice nips at my heels with every step. "You know I'll be waiting."

2

ATLAS

"YOU REALLY SHOULD BE A LITTLE MORE CAREFUL WHEN THAT fucking monster is loose in your house," Elara, my Partner in Knighthood, says as her slender fingers brush against my tender skin, causing me to wince, a hiss pushing through my teeth. The nick on my jaw is deeper than I thought, which explains all the blood that's splashed in the sink, the metallic scent filling my nose. "One of these days I'm going to come over here and find you either ripped to fucking shreds or completely turned and ready to eat me."

Turning my face away from her touch, I brush past her to the dimly lit hall. "He can't actually do anything, Elara, even if he wanted to," I say over my shoulder, stepping into the hallway. "He's all bark and no bite."

The fucking irony in my own words—*my lies*.

She scoffs as she follows me through the house, running her fingers along the wall and over the antique buffet, the pads of her fingers squeaking against the lacquer finish. "He's an actual monster, Atlas. Do you really think that little apotropaic marking carved into your skin is going to keep a fucking vampire from sucking you dry? He's far more powerful than you give him credit for, and he *needs* to be destroyed."

I glide my fingers over my chest, feeling the slightly raised skin that presses against my shirt. Even as my oldest friend and partner, she has no idea of the lengths it took to carve the signet into my skin and ensure the proper steps were taken to keep Emilian at bay and that he would obey my orders if his bloodlust were to take over. While we've had some close encounters, so far, he's never been the one to cross the line.

"As much as I loathe his existence, he's a useful weapon to have for my part in the Legion. And if the Grand Master saw him as a true threat to the city, he wouldn't be here." I reach above my head, pulling a white mug out of the cabinet. "Tea?" I ask over my shoulder, my fingers hovering over another mug, shifting the subject away from Emilian.

The barstool scrapes the floor as Elara takes a seat, running her fingers through her short, dark curls. She shows off her toned muscles, which push against her dark, umber brown skin, in her cut-off tank top as she rolls her broad shoulders back. The array of tattoos that dot up her arms and across her collarbones —along with her *fuck you* attitude—gives her an edge and makes her look dangerous to both humans and monsters alike. "Who are you, the Grand Master?" She asks with a scoff, crossing her arms over her chest and resting her elbows on the countertop. "How can you think of tea at a time like this? We're about to be out in the streets looking for a fucking monster, not settling in for the night."

A smile tugs at the corners of my mouth, but I bite it back, scraping my teeth over my bottom lip as I turn toward her. "We're looking for a *very* specific Gargoyle, and unfortunately, he's glamoured, so even his own kind can't sniff him out. And I think we need some caffeine to sharpen our wits."

I set the mugs on the large island, the ceramic scraping against the white marble countertop, and go about preparing the tea as she rambles on. "How can a Gargoyle be glamoured, anyway? Do they have that kind of magic? And—wait, don't they turn to stone in the daylight? Why don't we just follow him back to his lair, bust him up with a hammer, and call it a fucking day?"

A laugh tumbles from my lips, vibrating my chest—it's such a foreign sound that I almost forgot I could even produce one. "You don't think other Knights haven't thought about that? Plus, it can regenerate itself with other stones and boulders. You have to track it and destroy it in its glamoured form." She frowns, her brows stitching together. "That's just how their magic works. I don't make the rules."

I only know these facts thanks to Emilian and the research he's done for me. He spends hours studying the other beings that tear through the city, his stack of books only growing higher every time he raids the library, and earns brownie points to keep him in everyone's good graces. Everyone, that is, except for Elara.

She groans, leaning back in the chair, arms still crossed. "We don't have to take that *thing*, do we?" She scrunches her nose in disgust as she looks over her shoulder in the direction of the basement door. "I can't stand the way he's always watching me as if I'm his worst fucking enemy. Fucking leech."

Shaking my head, I pull the screaming kettle from the stove. "Not tonight. He wouldn't be much use against a Gargoyle, anyway. You know that whole thing about them not actually having any blood, but some kind of weird goo, and extremely thick skin? There'd be no point."

She rolls her eyes as I push her mug toward her, tendrils of steam rising and swirling in the air. "Then what fucking good is he anyway? He's no better than a muzzled bloodhound."

I blink, and the room falls away, pulling me into a memory that lives in the forefront of my mind.

I'm back on the brick-laid streets that stretch through the outer ring of the city, the frigid air slicing through me as I drop to my knees, the broken asphalt puncturing my skin. Pain shoots through my chest, burrowing deep and settling into my ribcage, as a dark laugh filters through the shadows shifting around me. Wrapping my arm around my middle, I fall forward, my free arm barely catching me. My bones creak as the pressure builds, the sound of heavy breathing getting closer as the monster closes in.

"Please." I barely manage to get the word out as the pain radiates through me, climbing up my spine, ready to devour my mind. Claws prick at my nape, and I squeeze my eyes shut, preparing for the end.

To die.

But it never comes. Only the sound of a snarl fills the air just as everything goes black.

I blink and find myself standing back in my kitchen, Elara entirely oblivious to my flashback as she blows on her tea while adding an obscene amount of sugar by the spoonful. I shake my head of the memory, not wanting to spiral any further or draw attention, and casually wipe the sweat that dots my brow, and quietly clear my throat. "He can kill almost anything else, Elara, but he's not fit for this mission. I don't want him out in the open if he doesn't need to be. And I know his limits."

Her eyes flash back to me as she quirks a brow. "Do you know yours?" The question grates on me as I grip the edge of the countertop. She has no idea the limits I've set for the last 10 years of my life that I've had to dwell with a blood-sucking monster living in my house, the lines I've been tempted to cross as I lay awake at night, listening for him, waiting for the day that he breaks through the wards and consumes me whole.

I lift the mug and take a long sip of tea, the hot liquid burning my mouth, settling me back to reality. I let the burn flow down my throat as I swallow, filling me with a temporary warmth. "What are you suggesting, Elara?" I sound almost hoarse as the hot liquid sears my vocal cords.

She's on her feet, rounding the island with a heated gaze. A crackle of electricity buzzes between us, and the energy in the room shifts suddenly, knocking the air from my lungs. I set my mug down just as she plants her hands on the counter, caging me in. "I think that you've been lying to yourself for a long time,

Atlas. And you've been too fucking scared to make a move." She moves in, her chest pressing against mine.

My heart skips a beat as I look down at her, fear attempting to grip my throat at the idea that she sees right through me—through my lies.

"Elara," I breathe, the strawberry scent of her shampoo filling my nose as I grip the countertop behind me, fighting the urge to grab her by the waist and let my fingers press into her exposed skin, my cock growing harder, pressing against my zipper. "W-what are you doing?"

She runs her nose up my jaw, bringing her lips to hover over mine. Our breaths mingling, and my heart racing. "Something that I've been waiting for *you* to do for years, Atlas. Something that I know we've both wanted for a long time." She presses her lips to mine, and I can almost hear the audible snap of her self-control as she wraps her arms around my neck, weaving her fingers into my hair.

Opening my mouth, she deepens her kiss while pressing her core against me. Her leg lifts to wrap around my waist, and I grip her ass as I lift her and turn, setting her on the counter. We shift, and I hear the sound of shattering glass as the mug hits the floor, but I can't find it in myself to care as I run my hands up her sides. I palm her breasts through her thin shirt, her nipples pebbling beneath my touch as she arches her back.

I groan at the thought of her parading around braless this entire time, waiting for me to figure it out.

You really need to get your eyes checked, you fucking idiot.

She begins to unbutton my shirt as I find the hem of hers to pull it up and over her head, breaking our kiss and halting her efforts. I look over the tattoos that cover her chest and trail down one arm into a half sleeve. Flowers, moons, stars, and a pair of snakes curl through each other, turning her into a walking piece of art. I lower my mouth over her tight, blush nipple, flicking my tongue as I gently grip it between my teeth. She gasps as she grips my hair, my name nothing more than a breath as it leaves her lips.

I suck and kiss on her breasts, moving between them, before finally lowering her back on the countertop. I admire her from where I stand between her legs, dragging my fingers down her torso. She's stunning and lethal as any weapon, with her years of training making her into the Knight she always dreamed she would become. We've stood side by side through countless missions, making our connection to one another undeniable. She is the moth to my flame, letting her wings become singed and charred as she orbits around me, putting herself at risk of becoming nothing more than embers and ash.

She props herself up on her elbows and gives me a knowing smile, palming her breast and tweaking her nipple. "Are you going to tear me apart with those teeth, Atlas?" Her voice has gone low, the sultry sound like nothing I've heard from her before. "Make a bloody mess of me?"

I brace my hands on either side of her as I bend over and nip her stomach, causing her to yelp before swirling my tongue over her sensitive skin. Her back arches as I work my way down to the waistband of her black leggings, grabbing them with my teeth and letting them go with a snap. Curling my fingers under the fabric, I tease her as I slowly pull them down, lifting her ass and making it easy for me to glide them over her thighs and down her legs, leaving her in only a black lace thong.

I can't help but lick my lips at the sight of her toned thighs and wide hips, letting my instincts take over as my cock twitches in my pants.

I tease her as I run my fingers along her panty line, brushing my knuckles over the damp fabric at her core. "Is this what you've actually been hunting this whole time, Elara?" My voice is a rumble in my chest, rattling my ribs. "Instead of the monsters we've vowed to destroy?"

She raises her head, her black curls framing her face as she looks down her body at me. "Oh, I've been after a monster, just not the kind that we talk about in the Knights' Circle."

I smirk, pressing a kiss to her pelvic bone and running my tongue across her skin. She moans quietly, the sound no louder than the squeak of a cathedral mouse, as I run my fingers up the inside of her thighs, her legs widening. I watch her squirm as I tease her, her pussy growing wetter with every stroke of my fingers, the smell of her desire filling my nose and making my mouth water.

"Atlas." Her back arches as I slide my hand under her panties and circle my finger around her entrance, keeping them in place and letting the fabric cut into her skin.

"You're so fucking wet, Elara," I growl as I lean forward, pressing my face to her center and taking in a deep breath. "And you smell fucking delicious." She bucks her hips as I slide a finger into her, slowly pumping it in and out.

"Then have a taste. I know you've been dying for one." She's breathless, the sound of her sultry voice making me hard.

My cock thickens as I watch my finger pump in and out before I add a second, stretching her. I nip the inside of her thigh, her moans of pleasure growing louder as I bend over and flick my tongue against her clit, her hips involuntarily bucking against my face at the contact. She tastes better than I ever imagined, and I let out a growl as I pull out my fingers and grip her hips, yanking her to the edge of the counter. I wholly consume her like I'm nothing more than a stray, lapping her up like the starved monster she claims me to be.

The one I know I am.

"I've been waiting so fucking long for this. For *you*," she moans as she reaches down and grips my hair, pulling me into her needy pussy as she climbs higher, finally coming undone all over my face. I rise and unbuckle my pants, pulling my thick, throbbing length out and pumping my hand over it, coating it in the precum that mercilessly drips from the tip.

"You're on the pill, right?" I ask as I continue to stroke

myself, letting my gaze rove over her body, noting every flex of her muscles.

She lifts her head and nods, her short, dark brown curls falling over her forehead. "I have an IUD, and I haven't slept with anyone since Troy. But don't worry, I got tested after he fucking cheated on me."

Ah, her piece of shit ex, who thought she was sleeping with me on our late-night missions and wanted to enact revenge by sleeping with an alleged bounty hunter, who isn't good enough to be a Knight. I have half a mind to sic Emilian on him, but maybe that was all for the best now that she has no strings attached to anyone else, meaning I have no excuse not to fuck her. Even as a tiny voice in the back of my mind tries to convince me otherwise.

Sliding my hard length through her folds, I coat myself in her cum. "*Godsdamn*, Elara. I'm going to fuck you until you see stars and scream my name like a banshee." I line myself up and slowly push into her, feeling her inner walls contract around me, pulling me in deeper and filling her.

Gripping her ass, I lift her as I pull out and slam back into her so hard the glasses in the cabinets rattle. She moans as I take her deeply, making up for all the nights we've spent hiding together in the shadows with brushing fingers and stolen looks.

She reaches between us and circles her fingers over her clit, and I watch her as she quickens her pace, moaning my name as her eyes flutter shut, her breaths turning shallow. My balls tighten as she matches my rhythm as I pound into her. She tightens around me as another wave of pleasure washes over her. She chokes out my name; the sound of it on her lips is enough to send me over the edge. I thrust into her and growl, digging my fingers into the lush skin of her hips as I come inside her, filling her and letting her pulsing pussy milk me dry.

Breathless, I lean forward and wrap my hand around her nape, pulling her up to me while staying seated inside her. Slanting my mouth over hers, I kiss her deeply, letting her taste herself on my tongue as her fingers weave into my hair. I pull away and drag my tongue across her jaw, sucking on the delicate column of her neck, leaving my mark on her skin.

I'm already hard again, my body thrumming, hungry for more. *Begging.* I pull her down and turn her around, pressing her face into the counter, her fingers curling into the stone as I deliver a sharp slap to her ass. But even as I lose myself to the ecstasy of the moment, I can't shake this nagging feeling—this quiet voice in my mind that sounds like it's underwater, screaming for me to bring it to the surface.

But instead of reaching for it, I push it further down, drowning it as I dive into the pleasure I've so desperately deprived myself of for so long.

3

ATLAS

THE MONSTER'S CHEST RISES AND FALLS FROM WHERE HE SITS propped against the wall, bound and chained just like I left him. The last stair creaks as I step onto the hard floor of the basement, face to face with the door of his enclosure. "I know you're not fucking sleeping," I say, scoffing. "The undead can't dream, anyway."

The silence hangs heavy on me like a wet cape; the only sound is the quiet clinking of the chain as he shifts from where he sits on the floor. As I shove the key into the lock, his voice floats through the bars, curling around me like a cat. "You smell like *sex*." He says the last word with so much disdain that it rattles his enclosure. "Like *her*."

I freeze from where I hold the key in the lock as my eyes flicker up where his red irises narrow on me. What am I even supposed to say to that?

Nothing, Atlas. You don't have to say anything to the vermin that infests your home. Your life.

Turning the key, the lock clicks, the sound as loud as dynamite blowing a hole through the silence, the ground rumbling beneath my feet. I slowly pull open the door and step in, my feet sinking into the plush rug that covers the hard floor, and watch him closely as I cross the space, taking it in. While yes, it's in the basement, I have worked to make sure that he's not living in squalor. The entire space is his, which is larger than most Knights' apartments, giving him plenty of room to live comfortably, even when he's chained.

Candle sconces flicker above his full bed, the brass headboard barely peeking out from behind the plush pillows, his duvet tucked under them. On each side is a wooden nightstand stacked with books, barely making room for his table lamps. A matching antique dresser and wardrobe sit on the far side of the room, filling the wall next to a bathroom I had installed when he moved, adorning a soaking tub, toilet, and small, mirrored vanity—per his request.

On the other end is a large reading chair with massive bookshelves framing it, a tall brass floor lamp warmly lighting the space. The shelves are packed so tightly with books and tomes he's acquired through the years. From where? I'm not sure, but he's slowly catching up with the collection in the study, even though he's constantly perusing through them with an insatiable hunger for knowledge that seems to run deeper than his thirst for blood.

I take another step closer and half expect Emilian to stand at my arrival, as he always does, as another way to get under my skin. But this time, he stays in place, his black eyes absorbing the light and snuffing it out, his red pupils narrowing on me even more.

"We took down the Gargoyle that was preying on sex workers," I say casually, trying to ease the tension pressing against my throat, as if it's a hand trying to suffocate me. "And almost lost my dagger in the process. Who knew Gargoyles were so fast?"

Emilian remains silent. "His glamour wasn't as foolproof as he thought," I continue, quietly clearing my throat. "Chancellor Karrn will be pleased to eliminate another rogue of his kind and put them back in the good graces of the civilians."

Still, he says nothing as anxiety prickles across my skin like a train of ants, their pincers digging in. I move a few steps closer, getting a better look at him with his legs stretched out, his head leaning back against the stone wall with his eyes tilted toward the ceiling.

"Did your beloved Chancellor give you permission to fuck that *woman* to ensure you would complete your mission?" He finally breaks his silence with his pointed words—as sharp as a knife to my throat. "Or was that your own enticing way to be able to surround yourself with such an insufferable human? Were you spilling your secrets into her as you ate her like the starved man you are, or did you just simply fill her with your cum in a failed attempt to find release?"

I stiffen before sliding my hand into my pocket and wrapping my fingers around the stake that rests deep in the pocket of my tactical pants. His words are meant to sting, to rile me up, but tonight I'm not falling for it. It's possible I crossed a line with Elara, but that's none of his business, and something I'll deal with when the time comes.

As Knights of the Vail, we're not required to remain celibate, but relationships between Knights are a gray area, and are case by case if they're exposed to the Legion. I've heard the Grand Master is willing to turn a blind eye so long as it doesn't interfere with our missions or cause a disruption among the ranks. Elara and I wouldn't be the first ones to sleep together, and we certainly won't be the last.

He scoffs at my prolonged silence. "You don't think I can't smell her arousal all over you, Atlas? The way it coats your skin and lips? Your *cock*? She's practically been dripping for you for years." He grunts, tilting his chin down and meeting my gaze. "And for a Knight who hunts monsters in the dark, you aren't very...*stealthy*."

Anger pulses through me as my blood heats, and I rush over to him, sliding my fingers under his collar and yanking him forward. "You don't have a fucking clue what you're talking about, *leech*," I growl the word at him, letting him feel it as it vibrates down my arm, my grip on him tightening.

His lip curls up, showing his razor-sharp teeth. "You reek of her. It's *disgusting*." This time, it's him who growls. "Not even the stench of the Gargoyle you apprehended could mask her scent on you."

My veins heat even more as a mix of anger and embarrassment rolls through me. A flush creeping up my neck, settling into my cheeks, and the tops of my ears. "You know what's *disgusting*?" I snarl. "*You*."

Wrenching my hand away, I tower over him, my breaths turning rapid and my muscles aching with the need to pounce on him, sink my teeth into *his* flesh. "You have been nothing more than a constant thorn in my fucking side, and it would be all the easier to kill you and be free of you for good."

He narrows his eyes, the glowing red surrounded by a sea of inky black, trying to find a fissure of weakness to land a blow. "Then go ahead and kill me, Atlas," he says with an eerie calmness. "Remove me from your life once and for all." He nods to my pocket. "You carry that stake with you, leaning on it like a crutch and using it as a constant threat. Why not actually do something with it?"

Whipping the stake out of my pocket, I crouch and press the sharp point to his chest, my other hand gripping his long hair and yanking his head back, exposing his collared neck. I let it snag his loose, billowing shirt that reveals his hard chest, pressing hard enough that his eyes widen at the prick of the sharpened tip, letting it singe his skin.

I could kill him now and be done with it—with *him*. I could end this ridiculous bargain once and for all, freeing myself of the constant itch under my skin and my leaping, unsettled heart. His musky aroma fills my nose, moving up and wrapping itself around my mind like a snake, my body relaxing as it takes over.

No.

That's what he wants: to trick me into a false sense of security. That's what fucking vampires do—lure you in, and once you're in their clutches, they drain you dry.

"You're an atrocity to this world," I whisper, bringing my face closer to his. "A *damnation*."

He watches me, his voice slippery like oil. "And yet, here you are, ever the noble Knight. Housing me. *Feeding* me." His eyes flash to my shoulder before flicking back to my face. "Did she see it? The proof that you are betraying the very Legion you swore allegiance to, all for the likes of a monster? Or are you still hiding your true self from them and continuing to make your feeble attempts to mask your desires?"

His gasp rings out as the stake tears through his shirt, pain gripping his expression as he bares his fangs. The sound of sizzling skin crackles between us. I look at the slash across his chest, dark blood seeping into his shirt, his skin turning black at the edges as it already tries to stitch itself back together.

I reach down and grab the O-ring of his collar, yanking him to his feet and slamming him against the wall. The pain in his eyes is fleeting as he narrows them on me, trying to reach out and grab my soul as his red irises flicker. "You're scared," he says quietly, his head cocking to the side—the words sharp as fangs, trying to sink into me and tear me open.

"I'm not fucking scared of you. You're my fucking *pet*." I let the rage take hold; my hand shakes so hard that the chain he's attached to rattles. "And pets can be put down."

"I know you're not afraid of *me*, Atlas. You're afraid of the *truth*." My mouth gapes, and I attempt to spit my denial, but nothing comes out. "You're afraid of who you really are."

My breathing becomes erratic as I press the stake to his neck, dark blood welling from under the tip. "You're done speaking, Emilian. You think you can just use your allure on me and watch as I come undone at your whim?" I can barely catch my breath as his sandalwood and amber scent wraps around me, pulsing through me and filling my lungs to the brim. "That you can bring me to my knees and devour me like a feral beast?"

The edges of my vision turn red, but even in my tight grip, he remains calm, which only infuriates me more. I'm one of the top-ranking Knights in my Legion, with honors attached to my name, and he should be terrified of what I'm capable of.

His gaze flicks down to my chest and drags back up as he smirks. *Fucking smirks.* "My allure doesn't work on you, Atlas," he says coolly. "That was part of the bargain, remember? That's why we carved the insignia into your flesh—to protect you from me, unless you were willing to give me the things that we both so *desperately* crave."

He juts his chin forward, a sharp edge of his muzzle catching my lip, tearing the skin and filling my mouth with the familiar metallic taste. "You can blame me for all your proclivities, but we both know you're simply a liar. You've been lying to yourself and everyone around you. Lying about who you are and *what* you are."

I breathe him in deeply, my nostrils flaring as I pull him even closer, letting the blood dribble down my chin, causing his pupils to widen. "And what am I, exactly, *vermin*?"

He licks his lips and widens his smirk, the tips of his sharp incisors glinting in the low light as they elongate. "You tell me, *sire.*"

Yanking the stake away, I shove him hard against the wall as I step back, my blood boiling over with the rage that only he can elicit from me. "You don't know shit about me, you piece of filth," I growl. "And you *never* will. In fact, you'll stay down here, and you'll fucking *starve*. You'll live with your insatiable hunger for all *eternity*, and I will continue with my life and leave you for the next poor soul to discover when I am finally freed from you in death. I *hate* you and your miserable fucking existence."

Turning on my heel, I storm out of the cell—slamming the door behind me; the metal bars rattling as the door clicks shut. I ascend the stairs, my boots pounding with every step, even as the quiet voice in the back of my mind whispers for me to go back and check the door—check on *him*. But he's not going anywhere, not while he's chained to the fucking wall and fully muzzled. And even if he does, it won't be any skin off my back.

In fact, it would be the perfect opportunity to escape this bargain by reporting him to the Knights as another monster that's stepped through a rift, or tell them that he turned on me, and let someone else deal with him.

Let them trap him, kill him, and rid me of him once and for all.

4

ATLAS

I FILE INTO THE LARGE CATHEDRAL, MY GAZE DRIFTING UPWARD TO the arches as I admire the grand architecture that leads to the peaks gleaming in the light of the massive chandeliers. The stained-glass windows stretch up the walls, letting in the bright moonlight and illuminating their depiction of each Legion's crest. The mahogany pews, firmly bolted to the limestone floors, are already filling halfway back with current Knights, while recruits sit in the high balcony overlooking the main floor.

I adjust the lapel pin on my jacket, my gaze drifting around the room to take in the faces of humans, monsters, and other beings—all proud members of the Knights of Cindervail. The monsters and beings have lived among humans for ages, hiding behind glamours and blending in with their humanoid skin. Now, as the veil grows thinner, more vile creatures from the depths of Hell push through the cracks and wreak havoc on the city. It feels like they're lurking just out of sight, waiting for the wards to fail so they can take over and expose us to the crumbling world outside our borders. A chill prickles at the back of my neck as I imagine their hungry eyes watching, patient and relentless.

Despite that, we've managed to form a single Legion—a

unified force vowing to protect this city and destroy those determined to create anarchy. Meanwhile, evil continues to press against the wards, clawing at them, searching for a way in. The wards confine both them and us. But lately, with the rift growing and its location constantly shifting, the old magic is barely strong enough to hold as bigger, more vicious monsters—creatures that haunt my worst nightmares—slip through more often now, only making our workload heavier. The tension is constant, a low hum in my chest that never quite goes away.

Cindervail, though full of magic and largely isolated from the rest of the world, is no different from any other city. The wealthy live in high-rise buildings downtown. The middle class resides in commutable neighborhoods just beyond the skyscrapers, and the lower class lives in the old boroughs and on the outskirts, separated from the city by a dense forest and a river-like moat. The wards are just beyond this barrier and are constantly maintained by various groups around the city.

The forest teems with wild animals and monsters, running free and testing the limits set for centuries. A few packs of wolf shifters keep them in check while guarding the ward against demons on the other side, where their howls echo through the trees at night, a reminder that even guardians can be monsters.

I scan the faces around me and can't help but wonder how many of us truly feel safe behind these wards—or if we're all just pretending, choosing to live in ignorant bliss even as the constant battle to contain them rages around us. The thought lingers, a cold weight in my chest, as I tighten the pin a little more and focus on the large altar at the front of the room.

"Seat taken?" a familiar voice says from the aisle. My gaze cuts to Elara from where she stands over me, her eyes sharp with disdain. "Or are you saving it for the reason why you haven't returned my calls in three days?"

Shit. "Elara, I—"

She raises her hand, cutting me off as she brushes past my legs and lowers herself into the open spot next to me. Her body is tense, making sure not to touch me. A large man with wolfish eyes slides in from the other side, but he skips any pleasantries and keeps his eyes straight ahead, even as the tension between Elara and me increases.

"Elara, let me—"

Once again, she cuts me off with a flick of her wrist, gives me a sidelong glance, and forces me to sit in silence as the crowd moves around us. The chatter is a constant hum that echoes in the rafters. She only sits with me, so it doesn't raise questions from the other Knights, since it's an unwritten rule that partners sit next to each other—a sign of unity and respect

Fuck me.

I scrub my hand over my face and breathe out slowly. I should at least explain why I ghosted her and why it's not a good idea for us to be anything more than we were before, which now seems damn near impossible. I need to tell her I was spiraling and needed to be alone, locked away in my room, far from everyone—especially him. But telling her the truth could open up a bigger can of worms and might ruin things even more than I already have.

I listened to my dick that night and thought that it was what I wanted—*needed*—to rid myself of the other thoughts that plague my mind. But clearly, it wasn't. Even though we took down the Gargoyle with ease, I was distracted the entire time. The simple brush of her shoulder against mine sends a curl of nausea, the smell of her shampoo making my eyes sting as though I've been doused with tear gas.

This is not how I should be feeling after I fucked her twice in the kitchen and once in the library, where, after, she paraded around naked before dragging me to the fur rug in front of the fire. I curled around her, letting her drift off before I slipped away to clean up and dress for our mission. I can't deny that it was some of the best sex I've had, but something shifted, and even as I stood in front of the bathroom mirror, I couldn't shake this feeling of doom that was pressing down on me, as if I just made the biggest mistake of my life.

Thankfully, we weren't called with any orders after we took down that Gargoyle, and we were given a few days off to recoup, giving me an excuse to avoid everyone without any questions. But I should have known better than to ignore Elara. We've always been able to work through our issues, but this time, I don't know if that's a possibility. I took advantage of her deep-seated feelings for me, thinking that I could recoup them, but instead, I'm left feeling even more of a shell than I did before.

The cathedral quiets down as a large man walks onto the stage from a side door, dressed in a classic tunic with the Knights' insignia stitched in gold across his chest—crossed arrows with a dagger pointed downward in the middle, encircled by a halo of vines with blooming blood red roses, their thorns pointing outward. The same insignia that each Knight wears on their uniform as a badge of honor.

Our Grand Master, Ransley, is over seven feet tall, with broad shoulders and ink-black hair pulled away from his face to show his sharp, russet eyes and reveal his pointed ears—highlighting his Fae origin. The last I heard, he was well over 500 years old and used to pass through the rifts between his world and ours until the veil to Hell split open, forcing him to close his access to the Fae realm and lock himself, along with a few dozen of his kind, here to create a haven as the rest of the world crumbled around them.

They stepped up as leaders, encouraging others to follow them as they fought back the monsters that were running rampant until the wards were complete, all while creating a new order: The Knights of Cindervail.

For centuries, Cindervail has been one of the only places in all the realms where humans and immortal beings have come together to stand united: to protect our homes and fight to find a way to close the rift in the veil permanently, which would possibly allow them to lower the wards and open the city back up. It sounds like an impossible dream, but one that we've been working toward this entire time—a chance to finally be free from our confinement.

The creak of the pews and shuffling of feet pull me from my thoughts as the crowd stands in respect for Ransley and the high-ranking officers who have followed him onto the stage. We all bow together, placing our hands over our hearts and pressing our palms against signet pins, each representing our different Legions and their Chancellor.

I press my fingers against the tips of the horns that extend beyond the roses and thorns of my Legion's crest, which features a lit torch in the center, symbolizing the way back to the Vail. Our Chancellor, Brander, is a highly respected Minotaur who has battled hordes of demons all on his own in defense of the city for over 200 years. His brute strength is nothing compared to his intelligence, and his training regimen is so vigorous that only a few can handle the standards of being in his Legion. The next comparable is the wolf shifters, but they rarely let anyone other than their own in.

"Rise for the Vail." Ransley's voice rings high into the rafters of the cathedral, filling the room.

"Where evil will fall," we say in unison, straightening and looking to our leaders. Ransley nods his head, a ghost of a smile on his lips as he scans the crowded pews and signals the start of our meeting.

"Elara," I whisper so no one else can hear, but she doesn't bother to look in my direction. I bring my hand up and gently squeeze her thigh, but her leg jerks beneath my touch—just enough to force it away, but not draw attention to us. She throws me a sidelong glance that would ward off any demon before turning her attention back to the front. My hand hovers for another breath before I drop it away, and I turn my gaze back to the stage, pretending to listen as Ransley goes on with his updates about the latest hordes of demons that have entered the city.

"Come to my house tonight," I mutter under my breath, my eyes shifting in her direction. The large man on the other side of her glares at me with flashing eyes as he quietly snarls, proving that he's more than human. But even then, Elara doesn't take her eyes off the stage. Her body is rigid as she presses her back into the pew, arms crossed, as she huffs out a quiet breath through her nose.

I let out a long sigh as I settle against the pew, trying not to think about the vampire that I've left alone in my basement for the last three days. I blink slowly, attempting to clear the image of myself standing in front of the basement door, my body trembling as I fight the urge to rush down to the parasite that has done more than sink his teeth into me. He's infected my mind like the disease he is and constantly has me feeling like I'm in a fucked-up fever dream—a lucid existence.

He claims that his allure doesn't affect me, but vampires are known to lie and deceive to get what they want. They politely ask to come into your life before ruining it for the rest of eternity. Emilian's no different. There's a reason why only a handful of vampires are permitted to live here, but only ones who have walked this world for centuries. They created their own coven at the edge of the city, in a mansion, where they've lived peacefully, with the promise of not turning anyone and having complete control over their instincts.

The rest of the filthy bloodsuckers fled before the wards were erected, not wanting to be trapped and possibly captured or killed. Emilian is *literally* kept on a tight leash for this reason, because even though he is bound to me by magic and law, there are plenty who would gladly heave a stake through his heart as a form of justice—all of them in this room.

I watch Elara sidelong, a half-assed explanation pressing against the back of my clenched teeth, knowing that the whole truth would wreck her. She deserves to know that I genuinely care about her, not only as a Knight, but as a friend. And the sex? The sex was better than I could have imagined. But even seeing how easy it would be with her—our lifetime of history—there's still a nagging feeling in my chest, one that wraps around my lungs and squeezes out the air as it attempts to pull me under.

But no matter how much I rack my brain, I can't pinpoint what it is, and it's driving me to the edge of insanity.

The crowd claps, bringing me back to reality, and I look around, but instead of the meeting coming to an end, one of the Chancellors, an Orc named Cadogan, begins his spiel about whatever has been happening in his sector—I couldn't give a shit.

I press my nails into my palms to help me stay focused, but with every blink, all I can see is a pair of red irises, floating in pools of inky black voids, staring back at me through prison bars.

MY FINGERS CURL around the stake in my pocket, where I run the pad of my thumb up and down its smooth length, fidgeting as I make my way back to my townhouse. The clouds roll past the moon, my breath filling the air in front of me from the crisp evening as winter slowly presses in—the seasons changing quietly.

Elara left the meeting without a word, sliding past the large man on the other side of her and disappearing into the crowd before I could even get to my feet and attempt to chase her down. It's only a matter of time before she unleashes on me, giving me an earful about what a selfish prick I am, and how all I ever do is push everyone away.

And for that, she'd be right.

It's no secret that my circle of friends is small, and those whom I trust with my life are even smaller. I'm very selective about whom I share anything with, but Elara is a social butterfly, and the only way anyone could deny her beauty is with their eyes closed. She might very well choose to end our partnership as Knights—which would require us to be assigned new ones—and even with a decent replacement, I'll be the one left a little lonelier. She'll continue to thrive and move on with her life, leaving me behind in the dark.

It's also apparent that most people keep their distance from me. Once word got out about Emilian and how I was bound to keep him as a pet, the tone of the entire Legion shifted. I could hear whispers in the other clubhouses, with rumors that I allowed him to hunt the streets for his next victim and use him to gain status with Ransley. After a while, it settled down, but then I became a myth to recruits, making me sound like one of the monsters that stepped through a rip from Hell with his pet in tow.

If only they fucking knew.

My legs feel as if bricks are weighing them down as I trudge up the stone steps to the front door of the three-story townhouse. The brownstone looks nearly black in the darkness, with the bright limestone steps and corner accents gleaming. My eyes scan across the dark windows to my neighbors, where their lights shine through sheer curtains, illuminating the silhouettes of the happy family inside as they move around.

They've lived in their townhouse for almost as long as I've lived in mine. When we cross paths, they're always friendly, but I can't help noticing the sadness in their children's eyes as they play in their small, fenced-in garden, watching me sidelong. Maybe they think I'm lonely in this big house—but loneliness isn't my problem. Not when there's a monster lurking beneath the floorboards, testing me every night.

My keys quietly jingle as I pull them out of my pocket, and I peek down the narrow alley between our houses, checking to see if anyone is lying in wait, but there's only a white cat sitting atop the metal trash can, peering back at me. My boots scuff with every step, and I scrub my hand over my face while sliding the key into the lock and stepping through the door into the thick silence. Shutting the door behind me, I toss my keys onto the entry table, the metal sliding against the polished wood. I lock myself inside, the sound of the deadbolt like thunder as it echoes through the large foyer.

I lean against the thick wooden door, sliding down to the floor as the weight of my situation bears down on me. I groan loudly, curling my knees up and resting my elbows on them, dropping my head forward, my chin pressing into my chest.

How could I be so fucking *stupid?*

I should never have slept with Elara; that was reckless, especially since we're partners who pledged to protect each other. In a mission, I would defend her with my life. But romantically?

It becomes even clearer that I was thinking with my dick and trying to drown out the chaos in my mind, all while warming the little bastard. While the Chancellors will turn a blind eye and force us to figure it out ourselves, I have no doubt it'll cause an even bigger divide between the other Knights and me.

What good am I if they think I'm just trying to get close to my partner, playing the long game, only to finally fuck them and then quietly ask for a new one? Even without the vampire lurking in the shadows of my life, my reputation is going to go to hell once the rumor mill starts turning.

They can just call me Atlas, the partner-fucking, vampire wrangler.

I'm sure Brander will be proud.

"So. Fucking. Stupid," I mutter, hitting my head on the door with every word. I pull out my phone and pull up Elara's contact, forcing myself to call her before I chicken out. It only rings once before sending me straight to voicemail, proving that she's, in fact, ignoring me. And like the pathetic fucker I am, I leave a message. "Elara, please call me. We need to talk. You know where to find me."

I end the call and let my hand drop to my side, allowing the phone to slip from my fingers and clatter onto the hardwood floor. The grandfather clock in the dining room rings out, ominously filling the house with its bell tolls. Even though I know the time, I count the chimes, trying to calm my racing thoughts. "8...9...10...11." After the last toll rings out, the house falls silent.

I rise to my feet and head to the kitchen, passing the basement door as I do every day. But this time, I tell myself there's no reason to go down there tonight, that I need to sleep and figure out how to smooth over this huge rift I've caused with Elara. However, my eyes drift in that direction, and I stop my steps, my blood running as cold as the breeze that swirls up from the basement, seeping through the door that's been left cracked open.

5

ATLAS

I stare at the heavy wooden door, my heart racing as my vision tunnels. Could I have been so careless and left it open?

No, that's impossible. I always shut it and lock it tight.

Except…

I glance over my shoulder and notice that the kitchen light above the sink is on as usual; however, that doesn't explain why every sconce that usually shines to illuminate the hallway is barely aflame, as if someone dimmed each one as they stalked through the hallway. My eyes follow the shadows, searching for anything out of the ordinary, but everything is eerily still and quiet.

I take a breath, trying to steady the rattling of my ribs as my heart beats against them, and I catch the stale air in my lungs. A musky scent assaults my nose—one I'm all too familiar with.

I slide my hand into my pocket, pull out the stake, and let my arm drop to my side. I take a steadying breath, trying to prevent anything lurking in this house from sensing what they might interpret as fear, when in reality, anticipation pulses through my veins. The innate thrill of the chase—the hunt—makes my blood feel as if it's thrumming with magic.

I swallow Emilian's name as it rises up my throat, driven by the urge to yell out for him and demand he show himself, but all that escapes is a quiet huff, almost a growl.

While I believe he left the basement on his own—and I genuinely think he did—there's also a chance someone else could have entered, especially if they caught wind that the Knights were engaged in a long meeting. The Chancellors tend to ramble on about trivial matters, almost as if their goal is to keep us off the streets. It's noticeable that these meetings have not only become longer but also more frequent, and they're considered mandatory unless you've been given specific orders for the evening.

And I can't help but wonder, are they hiding something? Someone? Or maybe I'm just being paranoid — a result of living with a blood-sucking parasite who always has me on the fucking edge.

I catch a shadow shifting out of the corner of my eye as I walk into the dining room, pulling me out of my thoughts. Turning slowly, I tighten my grip on the stake in my hand and brace myself, only to see the flutter of the antique table runner across the buffet as the register below it blows out warm air, trying to counter the constant chill in the house.

I exhale and keep moving through the room, avoiding the creaky floors and not wanting to give any warnings as I approach the doorway and glance into the kitchen. The moonlight streams through the window above the sink, slanting across the island and dividing one side of the room from the other. My ears catch the quiet sound of a heel scraping against the floor, urging me to step over the threshold. Turning on the light, I brace myself again, only to find another empty room.

It feels like I've stepped into an intense game of cat and mouse, and I'm unsure of what role I play. I could easily go to my room, lock the set of bolts across the door, and hide away until morning. Or I can keep following the shadows through the house and hunt the monster lurking beneath them.

I've never backed down from a challenge, especially one from a fucking monster.

I turn the next corner and am greeted by another long, dim hallway. Only one sconce is lit at the far end, flickering like a beacon in the night. I slip my hand into my pocket for my phone to use as a flashlight, only to remember it's still on the floor in the entryway. "Fuck," I mutter as I roll back my shoulders and let out a steadying breath.

I make my way down the hall, one slow step at a time. I avoid the squeaky floorboards, stay as light as a cat on my feet, and make my way toward the back stairwell. If they're not on the main floor, then they must be rummaging upstairs. A floorboard creaks beneath my weight, and I quickly shift, even though I know it's too late. It might as well have been a blaring alarm in this deafening silence.

The door at the top of the stairs looms above, shrouded in shadows, giving it the appearance of a dark portal to hell. My fingers lightly curl around the railing as I start my ascent, my hand sliding upward with each step while the other holds my stake, the point ready for whatever is waiting for me. The only sounds are the soft tap of my shoe against the wooden steps and the pounding of my heart reverberating in my chest.

Halfway up, I hear a creak of a board above me, and I freeze; the sound is no louder than a mouse skittering across the floor. It almost felt intentional, as if whatever's up there is watching me.

Waiting.

I reach the door at the top and see that the dust that has accumulated on the brass knob for years is gone. I grasp it, turning it slowly, and just as I push it open to reveal what's on the other side, a loud banging fills the house, nearly knocking me off my feet.

I instinctively yank the door closed and glance over my shoulder as a deep voice calls out from outside, shouting my name in a panicked tone. I cautiously back down a few steps, keeping an eye on the door for anything that might crash through from the other side—a monster ready to sink its fangs into me. But it remains shut; the dust in the air settles back into place.

I take a breath and turn around to head back down the stairs. I swear I hear the faint creak of the hinges from the door behind me, as if whatever was waiting is taking a peek, but I don't dare look back as the pounding on the front door grows even more vicious, rattling through the house.

I rush through the house and into the entryway, where a silhouette fills the beveled glass of the front door. I hurry to open it, and even though I know better than to think it's Elara, I'm still disappointed that it's not her waiting on the other side, but another Knight—Jaxon.

He's a handsome, broad-shouldered Black man, his hair cropped closely to his head, revealing the glimmer of the scales that ripple across his skin. His serpentine eyes glow from being one of the few Basilisk shifters in the city. "Atlas," he says breathlessly, his hand braced on the doorframe. "Can I come in?"

"Jaxon." I step aside to let him pass, anxiety prickling my skin as I bend down to retrieve my phone from where it still lies on the floor and catch a glimpse of the barrage of notifications, all from him. "What's going on? Is everything okay?"

"I've been trying to call you." His words are clipped, panic and annoyance sharpening the edges to a fine point. "Have you heard from Elara?"

Her name strikes me like a slap. Jaxon is one of our close friends, but I doubt he knows that Elara is avoiding me. "No," I say, raising my phone as if it's evidence. "I haven't heard from her in a few days. Why?"

He runs his hand over his head, his eyes darting around the foyer, undoubtedly in search of Emilian. "I saw her yesterday at one of the clubhouses, and she mentioned she was going out on a mission, so I assumed she was with you."

My chest tightens. *A mission?* "I wasn't given any orders." I take a step toward him, but he turns on his heel and begins to pace. "Did she say where she was going?"

His hands are stacked on top of his head, and his breathing becomes erratic, a hiss between his teeth. "*No*. Where the fuck could she be? She would have been back by now. Wouldn't she?" I hear the desperation in his voice as he turns and spins, stalking back toward me, his pupils narrowing to fine slits.

I press her name in my phone and hold it to my ear, praying to anyone who will listen that she'll pick up. It rings all the way to voicemail, raising a red flag to the fact that she's been ignoring all my calls after the first ring, sending me straight to voicemail every time.

Something is really fucking wrong.

I end the call before the beep and drop my arm to my side as anxiety lays its heavy hands on me, threatening to drag me down to my knees. "Are you sure she didn't mention where she was going? Or who she was going with?" My mouth dries and my throat tightens. I run my hand through my hair and down to my nape, squeezing it.

He shakes his head. "No. She was *very* vague." He throws his arms down, his hands in tight fists. "*Fuck*."

His eyes flash, and his skin crawls as he threatens to shift. While my townhouse is large, my foyer isn't large enough to accommodate him in his Basilisk form. I raise my hands, backing away slightly. "Jaxon, please, hold it the fuck together. We're going to figure this out."

"Something's off," he says with a long hiss, his tongue darting from his mouth, already forking, and his eyes flash even brighter. "We have to fucking find her, Atlas. She could be in trouble."

"We need help." I scroll through my phone. "What if we called—"

"*No*." His eyes flash again. "You know that if any of the Chancellors find out that Elara went on a rogue mission, she could be exiled. Is that what you want?"

As much as I hate to admit it, he's right. Squeezing the phone, I click the lock button and slide it back into my pocket. "Well then, what do you suggest we should do? Wander aimlessly around the city and call her name as if she were a lost dog? Put up flyers on the telephone poles?"

Jaxon hisses, his eyes flashing with ire as he battles the urge to shift. I step back, running my hand through my hair and gripping the roots.

Where are you, Elara? Why would you go on a rogue mission? Why wouldn't you tell me?

A chill fills the air, and the familiar scent of sandalwood and amber wafts into my nose, setting the blood pulsing through my veins on fire. The foyer has grown eerily still, the kind that blankets over me at night as I stare into the darkness, waiting for the shadows to shift. I look at Jax, whose shoulders are squared toward the hallway, his hands curled into tight fists—a serpent waiting to strike.

I follow his gaze, and there, standing in the shadows at the end of the hall, are two red, glowing eyes tracking our every move.

Watching.

Waiting.

Ready to go on a hunt.

6

EMILIAN

THE SWEET SCENT OF BLOOD FILLS MY NOSE, MAKING MY MOUTH water as if it were one of the finest wines known throughout the city. The rich, metallic scent is unlike any I've ever smelled. It's sweet and *intoxicating*, drawing out a deep hunger and making me feel lightheaded. The gnawing feeling grips me as I walk through the shadows of the abandoned alleyways, dodging the cracks in the cobblestone streets in one of the old sections of the city that has been left to decay and crumble.

My body hums as I turn the corner, the smell intensifying with each step. I can feel the prick against the inside of my lip as my fangs slowly elongate, my cock twitching—craving a taste of whatever might be waiting for me.

A low growl drifts through the streets, mixed with the smell of brimstone, with embers seeming to float in the air. I slow my steps, pressing against the rough brick as I peek around the corner. Clouds obscure the silver moonlight, causing shadows to swirl through the abandoned streets. It's well past midnight, and the dilapidated houses are boarded up tightly, with not another soul in sight.

A large man in a suit—no, a *demon* that looks as though it's been dragged out from the tar pits of Hell—stands over a bloody human, laughing as it circles them. The demon is massive, its muscles rippling under its tar black skin. Its glamour is fizzling as its extremities form into claws and taloned feet, its spine bulging and pressing against its skin, revealing itself through its tattered shirt. Its facial features are grotesque, as if it's made of wax that was left to melt in the sun. Its lips are pulled back in a taunting smile, exposing its sharp teeth, while its onyx tongue slides over them, a gleam of drool collecting on the tip.

"What is a tasty little treat like you doing in a place like *this*?" The demon's voice is as slick as oil; the words dripping from its lips. Its shadows curl around the human, making it impossible to see just how much damage has already been done.

Blood pools beneath them, sweeter than anything I've ever smelled before. My instincts pull me to them, nearly lifting me onto my tiptoes as its claws sink into me and beg even louder for a taste as my fangs continue to elongate, pricking the inside of my lip. But I resist, fighting against the desire just as I have almost every day since the change, halting my steps.

The human gasps and yells in pain as he struggles to raise himself onto all fours, clutching his side as blood oozes between his fingers. The demon closes the distance between them, its long legs propelling it forward, and grips the human by the nape. "Go ahead, my little snack, *scream*. Your fear will only make you that much more delicious." The demon's jaw unhinges, its wide mouth with rows of sharp teeth ready to swallow the human whole.

I let out a growl from deep within my chest, a feral instinct taking hold of me as I step out of the shadows, revealing my presence. The demon lifts its gaze to meet mine, a cruel smile forming on its lips as it watches me stalk forward, quickly closing the distance between us. It shakes its head and chuckles, "You'll have to find your own snack, you little tick; this one's mine."

I remain silent as I raise my chin, my fingers gradually transforming into claws at my side, tingling with the need to draw blood. I take a few more deliberate steps, allowing the heels of my boots to click against the cobblestone street, echoing between the buildings and getting lost in the rubble.

"Did you hear me, you fucking parasite?" The demon bites out the words as the human in its clutches gasps for breath, trying his hardest to let out a scream. He's pale as his blood flows from the wound in his chest, his sweet nectar wasted as it streams between the stones.

My shoulders hunch forward and show my teeth as the demon sizes me up. "Is it a fight you're looking for, fledgling?" It looks down at the human and drops him to the street, where he lands with a harsh thud, the breath wheezing from his lungs. "Come on then, let's get this over with so I can fucking eat." Its words are meant to be a taunt, and instead of taking the bait and charging at it, I stalk slowly to the right, leading its attention away from the human.

Its eyes follow me, and it growls. "If you think I'm afraid of you, *fledgling*, then you're sorely mistaken. I could devour you in one fucking gulp. But if I wanted to eat trash, I would just go dumpster diving like the rest of your kind does."

Another wasted taunt.

I'm very aware that I'm the equivalent of trash in this city—this world. I was never meant to last this long as an illegal fledgling, walking solo in this city, making me more vulnerable to being mistaken for a rogue monster. If I'm not careful, I'll be caught and killed—wiped from this earth and stripped of this miserable immortal existence I was forced into by the sire who abandoned me.

And even though I've been fighting to stay hidden and as discreet as possible, I think that if death were to come knocking, I'd greet him and let him lead me back to the depths of Hell where I belong.

I watch the demon as I circle it, taking calculated steps. While it's strong, its glamour continues to fade in and out as its shadows swirl, struggling to disguise it. It's not as powerful as it lets on.

A breeze pushes through its haze, filling the air with the smell of sodden embers. If I'm not mistaken, it's nothing more than a low-ranking demon that slipped through one of the rifts that have opened in the city—so low, even Hell didn't want it.

*Pathetic...*just like me.

The demon lunges for me, the cobblestone cracking underneath the sudden shift in its weight. It's tired of waiting for me to make my move and is more than ready to rip me to shreds.

And while it's fast, I'm faster.

I sidestep it, its massive body crashing onto the street and sending rubble flying. It roars, quickly getting to its feet and attempting to round on me.

Too. Fucking. Slow.

My body moves in a blur, and I'm on its back, my claws tearing into its skin, shredding it into bloody ribbons. It throws its head back and roars, the putrid smell of its blood filling the air. I widen my jaw and sink my teeth into its exposed throat, ripping it wide open and silencing it. Its demon blood is like gasoline on my tongue, burning my throat and nose as I sink my fangs in further, nearly smothering myself as I continue to rip it apart, piece by piece.

Its claws nick the skin of my arms as it reaches behind it to grab me, which only makes me more enraged, eliciting another growl and sending another feral pulse through me. I drop from its back, spitting out the blood and gore as it stumbles toward where the human lies, falling forward as its dark blood runs in rivulets down its chest from its exposed throat.

Shit.

I dart forward, gripping the human around the waist, and drag him out of the way as the demon falls to its knees, where it lands face-first, right where we were just standing.

The thick shadows dissipate as the demon takes its last, ragged breath, clearing the air from its toxic cloud. I rise to my feet and approach it slowly, kicking it right between its glazed over eyes. I'm not taking any risks; I need to make sure it's actually dead and not just knocked out, trying to regenerate. I grip the demon by its long, black hair, and with the last of my strength, I rip its head from its shoulders.

I raise it high, blood draining, and throw the severed head back onto the ground. It lands with a heavy thud, tumbling across the cobblestones and stopping next to its lifeless body, which has already begun to smolder, with embers and ash floating into the air.

A cough cuts through the silence, and I turn, watching as the human once again tries to get himself up on all fours. He looks up at me, his eyes flashing with panic. "Stay—stay away from me." He chokes the words out as he tries to move away, gasping for air as he falls onto his side.

My brow quirks as I look down at him, noticing each of the visible cuts and bruises that mar his otherwise perfect skin. Being human is such a delicate thing. Death is always lurking around the corner, waiting for an opportunity to steal another soul.

He presses his hand to the wound on his chest, no doubt put there by the very demon he was up against in a game he was sure to lose had I not come along. I close the distance, keeping my steps slow so as not to startle him more than he already is— like a cornered animal. My mouth waters at the increasing scent of his blood as it fills the air, my instincts begging me for just one taste.

One. Single. Drop.

No. You've had your fill for the day, you fucking vile creature. Try to find the last bit of your humanity and help him.

I crouch and gently push his brown hair back from his face, my claws skimming lightly across his paling skin. His panicked eyes watch me as his pupils widen, his body trembling with an overwhelming mix of emotions, the smell reminiscent of a smorgasbord. He's far too pale, a river of blood flowing beneath him, careening between the cobblestones.

As a fledgling, I can't turn him into a vampire, but at the very least, I can attempt to help him.

I lift him into my arms; his muscles flex against me, his body lean yet solid, as if he trains every day. The smell of his blood continues to fill my nose as it drips between my feet, my fangs digging even deeper into the inside of my lip, my own blood now flowing across my tongue. I fight down every urge—every instinct—I have to devour him. He groans, the sound a tickle in my ear, and his breathing turns even more shallow as his endless stream of blood soaks our clothes.

This neighborhood is obviously deserted—abandoned for years after people fled their homes before the wards went up, fearing they would be trapped in this crumbling city. I scan each stoop, trying to find one that looks the least condemned, not wanting to risk hurting the human even more. Even along these dank streets, there's no way no one heard the roars coming from this sector. I land on one that still has curtains hanging in the windows, with most of the glass intact, and the front door still one solid piece.

I ascend the stairs carefully, trying not to jostle the human, yet he still groans with each step. I check the handle, and it turns with a slight hitch, the hinges creaking from years of rust as it breaks free. As I step inside, I notice the house is in decent condition but remains damp and decaying due to age and neglect. The counters are cluttered with old pots and pans, mugs resting beside a coffee machine, and plates piled next to the stove, as if the last resident left in the middle of making dinner—never to come back.

I gently kick the door closed behind me, not wanting to attract any more attention. I pick up the sound of footsteps echoing against the cobblestones, with whispers filtering through the air as forces move into the area. Soon, we'll be surrounded.

"Someone's coming," the human huffs, quietly coughing as I pass through the foyer and into the living room. "They must have heard us."

The sofa is a deep burgundy, the edges frayed with moth holes and cat scratches. The springs beneath the cushions creak as I lower him, sliding my arms out slowly, letting my fingers glide through the warm blood collecting in the fabric of his shirt.

"They can't find me," he exhales, his face becoming more pain-stricken with every breath. "If they see me like this with you, then I'll never become a Knight."

A Knight?

That would explain why a human would be out in the middle of the night, entangled with a demon. "How old are you?" I ask, repositioning him so he's lying flat on his back, blood collecting in the corner of his mouth, his lips cracking.

"Twenty-one," he wheezes, shifting slightly, his face scrunching into a wince. "I'm in the final stages of being a squire." His voice, though weak, carries a tone of pride, at least until the following words leave his lips. "This was supposed to be my final test. And if they find out that I failed, I'll be kicked out. And they don't offer second chances."

He watches me quietly as I turn away and walk to the powder room, his gaze like a hot iron to my back as I slide open the pocket door and search for something to help staunch the bleeding. "How old are *you*?" he asks, his voice trailing behind me through the house, swirling around my head and caressing my ears, heating the now-pointed tips.

"I was barely thirty when my sire changed me," I say over my shoulder, ensuring he's still lying flat and not tempting his own untimely death.

"How long have you been a vampire?" There's a sense of wonder to his question, as if I were some ancient being that is only mentioned in fairytales.

I continue my search, contemplating his question and how exactly I will answer. It's been so long since I've spoken to anyone that my tongue is having trouble forming words, let alone holding a conversation with a soon-to-be Knight of the Vail.

It feels as though it was just yesterday that I was caught between a brick wall and a stranger who promised me eternity, only to leave me for dead. Yet, at the same time, it feels like I've already lived a thousand lives in this city as I keep myself hidden away. Time, as an immortal, is fleeting while holding me at a standstill.

Tucked away in a small cabinet is a stack of cream towels. Although they aren't spotless with the wear of time, they've been sealed off from the dust that has settled in this house, making them better than nothing. "Fifteen years, yet I'm still regarded as a fledgling and seen as a *very* dangerous asset to the city." My voice is low, a mere rumble, as I try not to let it carry through the cracks in the window above me, possibly luring in the strangers that now roam the streets.

"And where is your sire?" he asks as I approach, his words wet with blood threatening to drip down his chin.

What a nosey little fucker.

"I presume he's either long dead or escaped through a rift. I haven't been able to locate him since the night he changed me," I reply, a hit of disdain in my voice. This city is only so large, and yet, he has seemed to slip through the cracks continuously. Though I have not dared approach the coven that resides deep in the forest, as I don't know who they've made alliances with, and I've managed well enough on my own.

He watches me carefully as I lengthen my claws and slide one of them down his tattered shirt, peeling it from his skin and exposing his severely wounded chest. He hisses out a breath between his teeth, his face scrunching up in pain as his fingers dig into the velvet cushion, his back arching slightly as a groan of pain lodges in his throat.

Fuck.

I take in the damage, my mind racing. It will take a long time for his mortal body to heal, and we don't have that courtesy as the footsteps outside grow closer, the sound of Death knocking growing louder.

"Press this against your chest as much as you can. I can't heal you, human," I say softly as I hold out a towel, trying not to cause him any panic. "But the least I can do is take the pain away for now."

He opens his eyes, revealing a hint of distrust in his glazed-over gaze, the loss of blood draining him with each passing second. "Is that vampire code for you're going to kill me?" He coughs on the final words, swallowing down the blood that pools in his mouth.

I slide the shirt further off his shoulder, revealing his smooth skin, and glide my fingers across his collarbone to the pulse point on his neck. His body trembles under my touch, and my cock twitches as a deep, feral hunger ignites in my veins as his now-thundering heartbeat drums against my fingertips. I lower my face into the crook of his neck, inhaling his sweet scent and letting it fill my lungs, heat igniting like wildfire in my core.

"*Please*," he says softly, his face twisted in a grimace. I'm not sure if it's a plea for help or a cry for me to end it all.

I grip his shoulders and press him against the cushions, holding him steady. "This will only hurt for a moment," I say, just as I widen my jaw and sink my teeth into his warm, delicious skin.

7

ATLAS

THE DARK SHADOWS OF THE MOONLESS NIGHT CLOAK US AS WE WALK the streets, ducking into alleyways and weaving through the outer part of the city. "Do you smell anything?" I ask for what seems like the thousandth time as I look over my shoulder, expecting a demon to jump out at any moment.

Jax looks at me sidelong as we follow behind Emilian, who stays silent as he stalks the streets. "I can't believe I let you talk me into this," Jax grumbles. "Elara warned me about your little *pet*, but I didn't imagine I would be out in the open with him, where any being could see."

Emilian's shoulders stiffen—it's slight, and not enough for anyone to notice but me. His hearing is impeccable, and even though he's quite a distance ahead of us, I know he can hear every word as if it's being whispered into his ear.

I look at Jaxon, giving him a clever smile. "He's muzzled for a reason, Jax," I say smoothly, dulling the edge that's usually in my voice when Emilian is around. "Why are you so worried about him, anyway? Don't you have fangs of your own?"

I try to keep my tone light, but the tension weighs heavily in the air. Jax scoffs, "Fuck you, man." He sweeps his vision across the empty street, using his own means of tracking prey, his jaw tensing as his skin shifts to show off his glittering scales. "What happened with you and Elara, anyway?" he asks, his serpentine eyes shifting in my direction. "She was very short, defensive even, when I asked her about you."

I keep my attention on the street in front of me, but I don't miss the way Emilian looks over his shoulder, and even from this distance, I can see the smug expression on his face.

Fucking asshole.

I contemplate my answer, because after me, Jax is Elara's closest friend. And if she wasn't willing to air our dirty laundry out to him, then I shouldn't either. But honestly, if she had decided to hang me out to dry to the entire Knighthood, I wouldn't have blamed her after the way I treated her. I was a selfish asshole, and she deserved better than that.

"Our last mission was a tough one," I say roughly. "And she wanted some space to rest." It's the only answer I'm going to offer him, because right now, I don't know whose side he would be on, and I don't need any more enemies.

I rub my hand across my chest, feeling the raised, jagged scar beneath my shirt, trying to soothe the ache that pulses through it. I can still see the hurt disguised as rage in Elara's eyes when they fell on me at the Roundtable meeting, her burning gaze nearly leaving my skin singed.

Jax watches me carefully, assessing my half-assed answer as if he's watching me take a polygraph, waiting to catch the lie. While Jax and I are friends, and I would proudly stand by him for any mission, we're not under the same Legion. And while we share a lot through the Knighthood network, he's not privy to our orders or internal affairs, which includes information shared between partners.

The silence lingers between us before Jax lets out a quiet hiss, his gaze narrowing on Emilian. "So, how did you *really* get your little blood-sucking pet, anyway? It's always been a mystery that no one seems to be able to solve, not even the best detectives in the city." Disdain coats his words as his serpentine eyes flash in my direction.

I remain silent, not bothering to look Jax's way as we pass through a narrow alley, leading us further from the city center and into the nearly-desolate outer ring. Most of the lower class who still reside here are humans whose families have been killed by the monsters and rogues that tear through the rifts, leaving them with just enough to get by. This neighborhood is condemned chiefly and resembles the one where I once found myself near the brink of death.

"*Well*?" Jax pushes, keeping his gaze fixed on Emilian.

I huff out a breath, watching as it fills the chilled air, curling up and disappearing with the wind. "Like I've told you and everyone else, I found him in a neighborhood, just like this one, while I was out on my final order as a squire," I say, not taking my eyes off the street in front of me. "The Grand Master's ancient face nearly cracked with a rare smile when I arrived with the head of a demon and a chained vampire in tow. It was the Cindervail jackpot—two for the price of one."

"Your story is almost that of an urban legend," Jax says flatly, his curiosity seeming to turn sour. "Where, no matter what way you lay it out, it still never quite adds up."

My muscles tense as my neck flushes from where it hides under my jacket. At the same time, Elara has always been curious about that night, Jax has been relentless. He has been pushing me for years, with his own family even making offhanded comments that a human conquering a demon *and* capturing a vampire is something you read about in fantasy books. In fact, they've been the main ones to continue to raise questions, even after an investigation was conducted on the legitimacy of my claim, which Emilian ensured would tell the story we wanted. And so far, it has.

However solid my story is, though, the Basilisk's ability to see through my lies is almost as impressive as their thermal vision. Jax's family has served as Knights of Cindervail for generations, with his uncle being the long-serving and highly respected Chancellor of Jax's Legion, making Jax an early pick when we were inducted at the accolade—continuing his family's legacy.

But even if I am lying through my teeth, he's attempting to corner me about it for what seems like the millionth time, and it's time he let it the fuck go.

I halt in my tracks and turn to face him, my fingers curling into fists as my anger flares. "Are we here to find Elara, or did you drag me from my home on false pretenses so that you could interrogate me on what was an open and shut investigation nearly a decade ago?" I look around, gesturing to the empty street. "Did someone fucking put you up to this?" *To get back at me?* "Or are *you* questioning my loyalty to the Knights? To the city?"

Jax narrows his eyes, his gaze flickering over my shoulder, clocking Emilian, before sliding back to mine. "No," he says curtly. "I came to you because it seemed really fucking strange that the two of you went on a mission, and then, according to her, you went M.I.A. until we all saw you at the Knights Table meeting. Now, Elara is supposedly on a mission with someone, who I assumed was you, and I find out that she's actually been missing for days?" He squares his shoulders and closes the space between us. "Seems awfully suspicious, Atlas. *Damning*, even."

My fingers curl tighter, and I roll back my shoulders, ready to land a fist before he can shift and strike me. His eyes flash, narrowing his pupils to slits as he looks past me. The cold air swirls just as I feel a presence at my back, one that has haunted me every day for nearly a decade.

Jax takes a small step back as if he's been pushed, his brows stitching together, but in a blink, his demeanor shifts—*softens*. "I'm sorry," he huffs, running a hand over his head. "I don't know what's come over me. I'm just worried about Elara, and your little blood sucker has me on fucking edge. I really don't know how you do it."

The cold air is thick as we stare each other down. My confession fills the back of my throat, but I swallow it down. "You get used to it," I say flatly, looking over my shoulder at Emilian and giving him a warning glare. He licks his lips as he takes a slow step back. The chill in the air fills the space between us, as if he's stolen all the warmth from my bones. I glance back at Jax, narrowing my eyes at him. "Now, are you here to help, or do I need to do this without you?"

Jax looks between Emilian and me, noting the distance, and curtly nods. "I haven't been to this part of the city in ages," he says quietly, as he looks around at the condemned buildings. "Gives me the fucking creeps."

We keep going, Emilian light on his feet as he continues to move silently through the shadows. His grace is entrancing, and I find myself watching him instead of scanning the area. His long black hair flutters behind him in the wind with his leathers stretched tight over his muscles like a second skin. Seeing him out in the world, on the hunt, sends a pulse through me that warms my chest while prickling my skin with goosebumps.

"Atlas," Jax says in a hushed voice, pulling me from my trance as he picks something up off the ground. "Look."

He hands me a gold chained bracelet, dotted with tiny, teardrop-cut rubies, the same one that Elara has worn for years —a gift to herself for being dubbed a Knight, one I helped her pick out from the pawn shop. I hold it up and watch as it twinkles in the dim streetlights like tiny droplets of blood.

We both look around as if she'll come out of the shadows, declaring that this is nothing more than a game of hide-and-seek and payback for me being an asshole. Instead, I catch Emilian standing at the bottom of a stoop a few houses down from where we stand, his body rigid as he stares at the flaking red door.

Emilian glances over his shoulder, his red irises bright as he stares at me. "Someone's been in there," he says lowly, a growl forming in the back of his throat. "*She's* been in there."

Jax shoves past me, his shoulder knocking into me so hard

that I stumble forward, falling onto my hands and knees as the bracelet clatters across the cobblestone street. I groan while lifting myself, only to hear the hiss of a snake paired with the low growl of a monster—reminiscent of the one that lures me down my basement stairs, far beneath the floorboards.

Jerking my head up, I see Emilian has Jax by the throat, his claws elongating and pressing into Jax's molting skin as he attempts to shift. "You do *not* disrespect him," Emilian says with a deep voice that skitters across my skin and sends a pulse to my core, as he pulls Jax even closer to his face. The only thing keeping them apart is the muzzle that cages his gleaming fangs, which he has on full display.

"*Emilian*," I bite, keeping my voice down in case someone is nearby. "Let him go. *Now*."

I slowly rise to my feet, and he watches me closely, his heated gaze raking slowly up my body. "He needs to learn to respect those who wield more power than him, and who better to remind him of that than your rabid pet?" Emilian rakes his teeth over his bottom lip, letting his fang catch and slice open the skin, blood running down the corner of his mouth, staining his moonlit skin.

"He meant no disrespect, Emilian. It was an accident," I say roughly. "Let. Him. Go."

Emilian's jaw tenses, and reluctantly, he lets Jax go, causing him to stumble back while grasping at his throat. He hisses and turns to me, a stream of blood oozing from the punctures that dot his skin. "I'm going to kill your fucking pet, *Atlas*." He spits my name like venom from his fangs. "He attacked a Knight, which is a deed punishable by *death*."

I step up to him, our chests nearly touching as I gaze into his snake-like eyes, his scales dancing across his skin. "Too bad he's already dead," I retort. "And besides, according to Ransley, he's mine to deal with. So, how about you leave his punishment to me *after* we find Elara?" I turn on my heel, fully facing Emilian, with barely a breath between us. "*You* have a job to do. Don't get distracted."

Emilian takes a long step backward, watching me with red, glittering eyes as he bows low. "For you, *sire*. And for the Vail," he says coolly, rising back up and inhaling deeply. His chin tilts up, elongating his throat, putting his puncture wounds on display.

He spins on his heel and begins sauntering down the street as if he weren't just preparing to face off with a seething Basilisk. I feel Jax's rage as it rolls off him in waves, crashing into me.

"You good?" I ask, attempting to shift his attention back to me. He glances at me sideways and nods, rolling his shoulders back and once more running a hand over his head.

He stalks past me, his boots barely making a thud on the cobblestones as he keeps his distance from Emilian. I slide my hand into my pocket, gliding my thumb along the tip of the stake, reminding myself that I have the power. While I may not technically be his sire, I am the head of the house that was left to me. He might be a blood thirsty vampire, but he's my weapon to use—one that I am permitted to dispose of as I see fit. He crossed a line tonight with Jax, and I can't let that stand, because if I do, that will make me seem weak in the eyes of the other Knights.

A low growl emits from behind me, and just as I turn, I'm struck in the face. Pain lances across my cheek as I'm thrown backward, hitting the ground with a thud, sliding down the street. I scramble back to my feet, my head already throbbing and the wind knocked out of me, just as I come face to face with my assailant—a massive winged demon steps toward me from the shadows, its snarling maw dripping with black goo as it looks at me like I'm its next meal.

It's at least ten feet tall with mangled horns curling out of its skull. Its features are sharp, as its cheekbones sit high, and its jawline accentuates even sharper teeth. Its bat-like wings are twice its size; claws curling off the top of each one like spires from a gothic tower. The membranes scrape across the street as it moves, splitting eardrums with the sound of nails on a chalk-board. Its eyes are yellowed like a cat's, its pupils wide as it watches me in the moonlit night.

I take a step back, drawing my gun from the holster in my waistband—the same one that every Knight is issued at their initiation— and take my aim. The demon charges, its mouth wide open and baring more than one row of sharp teeth, its claws poised to swipe at me. With only a breath between us, I pull the trigger, and the shot rings out as a deafening roar slices through me.

8

ATLAS

I STARE DOWN THE FACE OF THE DEMON, A TRICKLE OF BLACK BLOOD coming from where the bullet grazed its shoulder, before I'm suddenly propelled backward as Jax shifts, his large serpent body plowing into mine, sending me flying. I slam into a pile of debris. Dust fills the air, blinding me, as a deafening screech pierces through the silence. The sound of stone crunching seeps through the high-pitched ringing in my ears.

I grip the garbage can that remains standing next to me and pull myself to my feet, my ribs aching. Jax has fully shifted into his Basilisk form, his fangs dripping with venom as he strikes at the demon, but misses as the massive monster flaps its wings, creating a windstorm of debris. The dust fills my lungs, and I stifle a cough as I stumble backward.

I watch as Jax is on the offense, continuing to coil and strike, but the demon stays just out of reach. Venom drips, sizzling against the stone street, seeping into the cracks. Jax's hiss swirls through the air, his eyes glowing a bright green. I reach for my gun and slide my hand over the empty holster.

Goddammit.

I turn and dig through the trash with vigor, a roar filling the air alongside a long hissing sound. With my back turned to the action, I sense someone approaching me, and I take in a calming breath through my nose, preparing myself for an attack. My fingers curl around the grip, and I turn, aiming it, Emilian staring down the barrel.

"I need you to remove my muzzle," he says, unfazed by the gun pointed directly at him, as he reaches up and yanks on the bars that enclose his vicious mouth.

"We're out in the fucking open. You know the rules," I say, still holding the gun at his face, the adrenaline making my hand tremble. I know these bullets won't kill him, but they would still do some damage to his handsome face for a while.

Where the fuck did that come from?

He snarls, his red eyes flaring as the tips of his fangs sharpen. "The rules don't apply when we're being attacked, *sire*," he growls, making the word as sharp as his incisors, his eyes flashing as he looks over his shoulder, his lips pulling up into a snarl. "Remove it. *Now*. Unless you want a replay of what happened a decade ago."

I lower my gun as I look past him to where Jax is dancing around the demon, gaining no ground in the fight and slowly switching to defense. I step toward Emilian, and he brings his hands behind his back, just like he always does to show that he has no intention of hurting me, standing as still as stone. My fingers brush against his long hair, the tendrils like strands of silk attempting to lasso my fingers. The buckle is cold as I loosen the strap, gripping it as it falls away, freeing his face from its cage.

Emilian's eyes flash, the whites turning black, his red irises glowing as black veins push against his skin, spreading out like a spider's web across his face. His fangs elongate, the points sharpening more than I've ever seen before. A gust of wind from the demon's wings catches his long black hair, sending it wildly around his head, making him look feral. His arms drop to his side, revealing that his sharp nails have grown into claws. This leaves his leather gloves in tatters at his feet, with his fingers curling up at the ready.

I stare breathlessly at the monster who stands before me. I should be afraid as his depthless eyes watch me closely, but all I can feel is a tight tug in my chest, trying to pull me closer to him, threatening to drag me down to my knees at his feet.

He looks as though he wants to devour me whole, as if he's on the verge of sinking his teeth back into my skin and finally draining the last of my soul from my body.

And maybe I'll let him.

The demon roars again, breaking the trance Emilian has over me, and I shake my head, staggering back and bumping into the trash can behind me, the sound rattling through the air. In an instant, Emilian pivots and places himself between the demon and Jax, causing it to hesitate just long enough for Emilian to launch his attack.

He leaps at the demon's wing, tearing it with his claws as gravity pulls him back down, landing steadily on his feet. The demon swipes, its claws grazing Emilian's chest and tearing open his skin as a roar erupts from him. However, he barely stumbles before lunging back at the demon, ripping into its other wing, shredding it like a thick piece of parchment.

Jax steadily circles them at the ready, giving Emilian enough distance to fight, while remaining close enough in case he needs to intervene. I watch as the two immortals battle it out, the demon's roars of rage shaking the ground beneath us and causing the decaying buildings to begin crumbling around us.

I hear yelling in the distance and turn, searching for the incoming Knights in the dust-filled street, but the sound of Emilian's scream draws back my wandering gaze. A sound that sinks into my bones and ties a noose around a deep part of me that I have kept hidden for a decade, threatening to yank it out. My veins heat with panic as I watch the demon grip him by the throat and hold him up in the air, shaking him like a rag doll.

"*Emilian*," I scream, the panicked sound foreign on my tongue. "Jax, help him!"

Jax hesitates as the demon throws Emilian at him like a cannonball; their bodies slamming together with a loud crack that reverberates through me. They're a tangled mess as the demon's gaze falls on me, its tongue sliding across the rows of sharp teeth, black goo dripping from its mouth.

It slowly stalks toward me, and in one swift movement, I raise my gun and fire, the silver-plated bullet piercing its chest. It roars in pain as the bullet lodges in its skin, the magic within vibrating as it forces its black blood out in rivulets, attempting to dig itself deeper. The demon's long tongue unfurls as it looks down and licks at the wound before reaching into it with its claws and effortlessly pulls out the bullet as if it's nothing more than a splinter. It examines the lump of metal before tossing it back in my direction like a coin being thrown into a fountain, making its wish to the gods, new and old, for my demise.

I throw myself behind the rubble and cover my head just as the bullet explodes like the ticking time bomb it was designed to be. Dust and debris cover me once again as I attempt to stand, with a slight ringing in my ears.

A clawed hand grips my hair and drags me back, the demon growling as it towers over me, its yellowed eyes narrowing. Bending down, its jaw clicks as it unhinges, ready to swallow me whole. I give it a cruel smile as I pull out the stake that has become a permanent fixture in my pocket and shove it through the roof of its open mouth, directly into its skull.

It roars, the sound seeming to echo around me as it bites down on my arm, pain lancing through me before it lets go and stumbles back, ripping out a chunk of my hair as it goes. It chomps its mouth, attempting to dislodge the stake, but only shoves it deeper into its brain. Another roar rumbles through the streets as the demon drops to its knees. It emits a gagging sound as black, tar-like blood cascades from its mouth.

Its face glows red as it begins to crack, and its eyes bulge as it claws at its face. Its body begins to tremble as it lets out another choked sound.

"*Atlas*," someone calls, but I'm too entranced as I watch an invisible flame consume the demon. Its skin slowly melts away from its bones as smoke rises and burns red like embers. And just as it falls forward, its head explodes, boiling, black goo splattering all around it, immediately eating away the cobblestones.

"Fuck you," I mumble as I drop to my knees, letting out a crazed laugh, adrenaline coursing through my veins. I look down at the torn sleeve of my shirt; the demon's bite is already festering, and the veins beneath my skin are blackening as they crawl up my arm. Panic rises in my chest, making it hard to breathe as I look closer at the damage. "*Fuck*," I choke out.

"Atlas," a voice says again, and I look up, meeting Jax's serpent eyes, but when he sees my arm, he gasps. "*Holy shit*. It bit you."

I look over to where the demon's body has turned into nothing more than a pile of sizzling tar, slowly seeping into the cracks in the street, dripping back to Hell. "I killed him with a stake to the head," I say calmly, even as I look down and watch the black veins work further up my arm with every heartbeat, disappearing under the remaining part of my sleeve. "It didn't like that very much."

In the blink of an eye, Emilian is in my face, gripping my wrist and pulling my tattered arm toward him as he looks between me and the wound. "What were you *thinking*, Atlas?" he growls. "You could have gotten yourself killed. We must get you home," he says with a lethal calmness.

"Are you *insane*?" Jax bites out, his forked tongue slithering through his teeth. "We have to get him to the hospital and let a doctor look at him. We don't know what kind of demon that even was, or how long we have before the venom takes over. Do you want him to fucking die?"

I laugh, even as my body heats and a sheen of sweat coats my skin, making me clammy. "I'm fine, Jax," I say, trying to stand, my head heavy, and my thoughts fuzzy. "It's just a scratch. See?" I hold up my arm, my darkening blood dripping at our feet like a goblet of spilled wine.

Emilian catches me by the arm as I waver on my feet, his red eyes narrowing on me just as he lifts and throws me over his shoulder with ease. He turns to face Jax. "I'm taking him home, and you are to mind your own business," he says coolly, taking slow, even steps as he walks away. "Go back to your home and stay there until morning."

"Atlas, tell your pet to take you to the hospital," Jax says from behind us, unmoving. "This is fucking insane."

"I'm fine, Jax," I reply as my head thumps gently against Emilan's back. My vision blurs as my body heats even more; my words begin to slur as my tongue thickens. "Emilian will take care of it. He knows what he's doing. I'll call you later, okay?"

This time, he's on our heels, shaking his head. "*No*, I'm coming with you. You're hurt, and I don't trust your little blood-sucking pet, especially with an open wound."

Emilian halts his steps, turning slowly to Jax, careful not to jar me as he looks around. "Someone's coming," he whispers, his voice carrying in the wind. "We need to get out of here. *Now*."

"I don't hear—" Jax starts, but quiets as the sound of voices carries through the alley behind us. "*Fuck*. If they find us, we'll have to explain what we're doing out here without orders. And how do we explain the Elara situation without saying that she's missing?" Panic begins to coat his words, his hands planted on his head as if it will topple from his shoulders.

"You *don't*," Emilian replies, his voice deepening. "Do as I say and go home. They will be none the wiser, as they'll be too busy trying to clean up this mess before anyone sees it." He swiftly moves in the opposite direction of the voices, gripping my thighs tightly as he picks up speed, taking us down an alley and cloaking us in shadows. My vision blurs further as everything gradually fades to black.

The last thing I see is Jax racing behind us, as if he were fleeing the scene of the crime.

9

5 YEARS EARLIER

EMILIAN

There's a quiet creak from above as dim light floods the stairwell, followed by boots thudding softly against the wooden stairs, careful to avoid the squeaky boards.

It's charming how he thinks he's being sneaky, as if I haven't been able to smell him through the cracks in this old house for years. My mouth waters as I imagine the taste of his blood mixing with his scent, my cock twitching.

I sit still as stone and watch him from where he stands at the bottom of the stairs, looking in at me like a child looking in the window of a candy shop. The only thing between us is the bars of my enclosure and these inferior chains, as I play the part of his pet. The muzzle he's affixed to me is quite the fashion statement, along with the other accessories that have been locked on me, etched with the symbols I showed him—my new sire as the bearer of the key, only to set me free whenever he sees fit.

Which is more often than he likes to admit.

"Wake up," he says with his low voice that has deepened as he has aged, a sweet tenor approaching decadent bass.

My lips curve into a smile. "The undead cannot sleep, remember?" I let my fangs elongate, the scent of him intoxicating as the most delectable meal, as he steps through the door, slowly closing it behind him.

"I'm well aware," he huffs as he approaches, his eyes heating —not with his usual ire, but something *more*.

I don't move, compelling him to step closer to me, his hand slipping into his pocket to grasp the stake he had carved just for me. There's a loathing in his eyes that burns for me, his fingers twitching at his side, his brows stitching together as his hair falls across his forehead.

He lowers himself from where he stands between my sprawled legs. His heated gaze rakes over me, pausing momentarily on my hardening length. The corners of my mouth rise even higher, my skin pressing into the leather strap that holds my muzzle in place.

"I know what you're doing, leech. Knock it off," he growls, his fingertips lightly brushing my thigh from where they dangle in the air, setting my skin on fire.

I shrug casually. "I can't help it, *sire*," I say, showing off my teeth, letting the word drip with amusement from my fangs.

"We've been over this," he groans, "I'm not your sire. I'm obviously not the one who turned you, I am just the one who... keeps you." His cheeks redden, but he doesn't look away; his eyes are burning bright in the dim light.

I observe him as his scent continues to envelop me, making me feel dizzy. "What else would you be then? You are not my master, as I'm not your slave—that we have agreed upon from day one. Nor are you a king, but only a Knight, and that fact alone says that I'm not your subject, though I do enjoy falling to my knees at your feet." His eyes sharpen, and he opens his mouth to speak, but I manage to get my thought in before a single word slips past his lips. "*Oh*, I know. You could be my *lord*." I let my eyes widen, my brows crawling up my forehead, before giving him a wink.

"You could just call me Atlas, you know?" he grumbles, annoyance in his tone.

I scoff. "That's far too casual for someone who hides me away in the cellar and keeps me under lock and key, as if I need protecting."

His face is mostly neutral, but I don't miss the way he slightly narrows his gaze. "Sire will be fine," he says curtly. "If it shuts you the fuck up."

"Very well," I say with a smirk. "What is it you need from me, *sire*?"

He blinks, seeming startled by my question. "I, uh, don't know, exactly."

"Did you...*miss me*?" I croon, tilting my head and letting my curtain of hair fall over my shoulder.

His face reddens as he shakes his head, his mussed hair sliding across his forehead. "I don't know why I bothered to come down here," he says quietly, yet he doesn't move; he only stares at me, a glimmer in his eyes as the tension grows thick between us.

I reach forward, the clinking of the chains echoing in the deafening silence, as I let my nails trace over the back of his hand, careful not to scratch him and draw blood. He stiffens, but still, he doesn't move, allowing me to continue tracing the veins that bulge beneath his skin and extend up his arm. His fingers twitch, yet he simply watches the movement of my hand on his. He takes a deep breath that seems to catch in his throat before shaking his head and letting his hand drop away.

When he finally looks back at me, his eyes have gone dark, and I have no choice but to lick my lips as I bring my fingers up to the cage of my muzzle to take a deep breath, breathing in the scent of him.

Delicious.

"Stop using your allure on me," he says, rubbing the back of his hand on his pants as if he's trying to scrub away my touch, but he remains where he's crouched down.

I chuckle, the sound as dark as the shadows in the corners of my enclosure. "Even if I wanted to, there is no allure strong enough to use on you. This is all of your own doing, *sire*."

He drops forward onto his knees, bringing himself a few inches closer. "I don't fucking believe you," he whispers, the sound rough as his voice drops into a deep growl, just how I like it. "You're always using it to call for me."

His hand floats up, gripping the chain that hangs around my neck, where it's clipped onto my collar—the same one that keeps me away from the door—as if a simple string of metal could stop me from walking right out of here. He pulls me closer to him, his nose pressing against my muzzle. "The longer you're in this house, the more I end up down here for no reason. You *must* be doing something to me. I keep you locked away for a reason, yet, here I am, still being yanked around by the throat as if *I'm* the one on a leash."

I flick my tongue out like a snake, curling it around my lips and raking it across my fangs. "Like I said, this is all your own doing. I am the one who is chained, muzzled, and caged. Nothing more than the pet you have declared me to be to your superiors. You are the one who is free to roam as you please, and yet, here you are." His hand trembles as his fingers curl tighter around the chain. "You used your own free will to come down here, *Atlas*," I say as smoothly as if I were to sink my teeth into the delicate skin at his throat, his name rolling off my tongue with a slight hiss.

The muzzle that rests upon my face is charmed and cannot be removed except by him; however, the chains are merely for show, serving only to provide him with peace of mind. They are nothing more than another layer of smoke and mirrors aimed to showcase power to his fellow Knights—a layer that is rapidly thinning.

He groans, running his fingers through his hair. "Forget it." He shifts to stand but stumbles, falling into me. I grip him, my hands landing firmly on his ass, holding him so he's straddled above me, his hands planted firmly on my shoulders. He stiffens, his widening eyes staring at me, flickering down to my mouth.

We are both suspended in time.

His warm fingers press into my skin, searing it as his breathing becomes shallow, the warmth caressing my lips. I watch the pulse point in his neck as it pulses wildly, beating like a war drum as it marches into battle. My gaze flicks up, and he is simply staring at me, his usual expression of contempt nowhere to be seen.

I slowly lower him onto my lap, my hands still firmly planted on his ass, feeling the thick muscles flex beneath my palms. I'm cautious, waiting for him to jump to his feet and charge out of here, as is his typical reaction when he's around me for more than a few minutes.

If I were still human, I might be offended by his response to me, but now, as an immortal, he is merely a blip in my timeline. It makes this game of tug of war with him that much more thrilling. But even knowing that our time is short lived, there's a bizarre pull to him that I can't deny. The feeling seems to grow stronger every day, making me more aware of his movements, counting the sound of his footsteps from above, and his intoxicating scent making my head spin as it fills the house.

I slide my hands out from beneath him, his ass pressing onto my lap. I slide them up to his waist, letting my nails sink in, anchoring him in place.

"Emilian," he breathes. "W-what are you doing?"

I shift, allowing my now-rigid length to press into him, but I don't dare move my hands, holding him as delicately as one would a baby bird. "Catching you from your fall," I reply, each word seeming to draw him in closer like a beacon in the night. "And keeping you safe. Just as I promised."

He lifts one of his hands, pushing my hair back from my shoulder, his fingers tangling through the sleek black strands. He sinks further onto me, as if he's settling in for the evening, his eyes widening as he shudders in a breath. "Are you hungry?" he asks, his words barely a whisper.

Licking my lips, I gently rock my hips, slightly bucking him up. "*Starved*," I say, a growl forming at the back of my throat.

His hands glide up my nape, his fingers curling around the buckle at the back of my head with a pace so agonizingly slow that I almost let the growl loose, my patience thinning as my feral side presses against my skin. He slips the leather through the buckle, the muzzle loosening before he pulls it away, dropping it to the floor at our side with a metallic thud.

I want to slip my fangs into his skin, let his sweet blood fill me and give me a buzz that only he can. But I remain still and let him take the lead. His finger glides over my jaw and down my throat, tracing the leather harness to my exposed chest. He continues to drag his finger around my exposed nipples, lightly flicking one of my piercings, sending a tingling sensation straight to my core. They were the last thing I had done as a human, and right now, it was the best investment I had made in my mortal life.

His hands slide away, and a pang of fear strikes my chest that he's going to leave—flee from me. Instead, he unzips his jacket, letting it slide off his arms before gently tossing it onto my bed next to us. His black shirt is pulled tightly over his broad chest, and it's hard not to notice how he has become physically fitter, faster, and stronger since being initiated as a Knight. While I'm annoyed and vastly worried by how much he is out of the house on missions, I can appreciate the hard work he's put in.

He pulls his shirt from where it's neatly tucked into his pants, his fingers curling around the hem before he lifts it over his head and tosses it on top of his jacket. My hungry eyes scan his usually tanned skin, which has grown lighter as he works more during the midnight hours and sees less of the sun, slowly becoming a lonely nightcrawler—like me.

I notice the delicate scars on his chest: one from the night he was ambushed by the demon that nearly left him for dead, and the insignia I carved into his skin to keep him safe in the end. I pass over those and focus on the deep fang marks that shine between his neck and shoulder, low enough that they wouldn't show through his typical uniform but perfectly positioned for easy access.

He leans forward slightly, giving me a clearer view of the scar I left on him all those years ago. I pull him closer, allowing him to feel every inch of me against him as he plants his hands on my exposed chest, digging his fingers into my pecks. He's lost in his lust as I lean in and run my tongue up the column of his throat, swirling it around his pulse point, the taste of his skin coating my tongue.

A shiver runs through him as I gently scrape my teeth across the delicate skin, careful not to break through, his thundering heart heavy on my tongue. He groans, lightly grinding against my cock, his body begging for more. I glide my hand up his side, taking my time as I scrape my claw across his nipple, forcing him to take in a shuddered breath.

Two can play at this game.

My fingers continue their exploration across his collarbone and back up to his throat, where my hand comes to rest against his prominence, feeling it move as he swallows thickly. I push my hand up, letting my fingers grip his jaw and pull him to me, his mouth a breath away from mine. "Emilian," he breathes. "*Eat*. Please."

I smirk as heat floods my abdomen, a tingle pulsing up my spine. "I will once I'm done playing with my food."

I run my tongue over his scars, working my way down to capture his other nipple between my teeth, eliciting a hiss from him. He remains stiff as he tries to combat the undeniable connection between us, and while he could end it at any time— slap my muzzle back on and leave me to starve with an eternal hunger—he doesn't move.

I glide my hands down his chest, his abs, and let my fingers hover at his waistband, observing his reaction as his length presses against the zipper of his pants. He shifts his hips, thrusting his pelvis toward me, along with a shallow exhale. I don't hesitate—undoing his pants with deft fingers, gliding his zipper down tooth by tooth. He swiftly lowers the waistband of his boxers, gripping his cock and rubbing his thumb through the precum that threatens to drip from the tip.

Gods be damned, he's fucking glorious.

His eyes lock with mine as he begins to stroke himself, his pulse thundering as desire overtakes him, both making my mouth water and my body thrum with need. I can feel my fangs growing longer, the whites of my eyes turning onyx as my deep, insatiable hunger rises to the surface from the dark abyss. But even as I transform into the damned monster I was forced to become, he doesn't flinch and never looks away, taking in the creature before him without a hint of fear.

I run my tongue over my fangs and widen my jaw, honing in on his shoulder as I align them with the delicate scars, not wanting to mar his skin more than necessary, even though all I truly want is to leave my marks all over him, claiming him as mine. I slowly push my teeth into his skin as he lets out another hiss, savoring the sensation of tearing his flesh.

His blood fills my mouth, and I let out a deep, guttural groan. His blood is like gulping down the sweetest red wine as I close my lips around him, sealing them against his skin. I take deep pulls, warmth flowing down my throat and filling my stomach, making my cock throb harder with need.

Atlas groans, tilting his head to the side and exposing his neck further as he continues to stroke himself, heightening his own pleasure as he falls deeper into a blissful state. I run my fingers through his hair, tugging gently while holding him in place. His hips start to rock against me as he finds his rhythm, countering my pull with each stroke of his hand.

It's been years, and he still holds out for as long as he can, afraid to embrace his desires and let us *both* have our fill. He wants to prove that he's someone more than just a man with skeletons in his closet and a monster in his basement—*a pet.* And while he's strong on his own, we're even stronger together.

His blood does something to me that no one else's ever has, and while I can't pinpoint it, I know we are nothing without each other. Although he may despise my existence on the surface, it is merely a façade—one that he's afraid to knock down and would rather keep who he really is locked up tight, ready to throw away the key.

Atlas's reaction to my bite is so visceral that it makes me wonder if he holds out for as long as he does just to fully immerse himself in the high that I give him. The lust warms his crumbling heart and soul while filling my undead one—bringing us both back to life.

I grip his ass with my free hand, pressing my claws into him, but not so hard to stop the movement of his hips. I sink my fangs in deeper, eliciting a deep, guttural groan from him, his desire dripping across my exposed abs. I keep my pulls slow, not wanting to take too much too fast. I'm not mature enough to turn anyone into a vampire yet, but as long as I control my urge to drain him dry, I will continue to mature like the other vampires that dwell in the shadows of the city. Then, when I find my mate, I can turn them so we can be together for all eternity, hiding amongst the shadows and moonlit nights.

"Emilian," he groans, the sound of my name on his tongue almost as intoxicating as his blood. I slide both my hands to his ass, roughly gripping him with my now-extended claws, gliding him back and forth, grinding him against me and working us both to the edge.

I can feel him getting closer, and I sink my teeth in just a little more, latching on completely. His head falls back, and he moans with a rough growl in the back of his throat that vibrates across my lips. His hot cum coats my abs, the sensation and his moans causing me to find my own release in my still-intact pants.

I grip him by the throat to hold his neck in place, letting him work through his orgasm until his moans quiet down to nothing more than shallow breaths. I slowly remove my fangs, running my tongue across the holes I left, licking away the last droplets of his sweet blood. His breaths are shallow, a sheen of sweat glistens on his forehead, and his eyes are clouded with lust.

I could live in this moment for the entirety of my immortal life; this relaxed and satiated expression that's on his face will be forever burned into my memory.

He looks down at the streaks of cum painted across my skin, his gaze catching on the dark stain of my own release in my pants. His eyes widen as he takes in the sight of his hand, still gripping his semi-hard cock before his gaze trails up to my mouth, the corners stained with crimson. I can feel the ground tremble as our delicate house of cards comes crashing down, scattering across the floor.

His hand slaps onto the bite mark at his neck, trying to conceal it from the world, as if it's pounding on the door and waiting for him at the top of the stairs. He's on his feet in a blink, hurriedly buttoning and zipping his pants before sidestepping to grab his shirt and jacket off the bed. His gaze lingers on the mess he made me, and I don't miss the small glimmer in his eyes that continues to keep me on a tighter leash than I already am.

Satisfaction.

But when he blinks, the gleam is replaced by his usual panicked expression, the one that emerges after he's succumbs to his own desires and blames the monster residing far beneath his bed for infiltrating the cracks in the shield he surrounds himself with.

He backs away, the distance between us once again pulling at my chest as if it were its own ball and chain. "I'll...I'll be back with a towel, and I expect your muzzle pressed against your face for me to put back on. You know the fucking rules." His voice cracks as he retreats to the bars of the cell door, stumbling past them and slamming it shut behind him. His boots thud up as he hurries up the stairs, the basement door slamming.

The room becomes completely dark again, lit only by the

eternal flames of the sconces, as if Atlas took all the light with him, leaving the silence to fill the shadows cast around me.

I took my fill and repressed the incessant hunger that gnaws at me, the one that has chewed a hole that I cannot seem to fill, no matter what I do. It's left me wanting—no, *needing*—more.

More of his blood.

More of his touch.

More of *him*.

IO

ATLAS

"WHAT YOU DID TONIGHT WAS FUCKING RECKLESS," EMILIAN HISSES from where he leans over me, examining the wound under the bright bathroom lights. "You could have gotten yourself killed, or worse, dragged to another realm, never to be seen again."

I slump against the vanity from where I sit on the floor, the burning sensation in my arm becoming even more agonizing with every beat of my heart. "I've managed to avoid death so far, and besides, another realm would just spit me back out like rancid meat," I say with my head tilted back, the white lights forcing my eyes closed. In the time it took us to get back home, the blackened veins had managed to drift past my elbow, slowly eating away at my skin, making my arm feel as though it's been dunked in acid.

Emilian looks up; his red eyes are fierce, and his exposed teeth peek out from his slightly snarled lips. My gaze drops to the muzzle that lies on the tile floor next to us, and while I know I should have already put it on him, I leave it be. I've been a fucking asshole and haven't let him out to feed in what feels like weeks, but if he wanted to kill me, he would have done it that first night we ever crossed paths. Ironically, I've been helping him learn to control himself through the years, even if his gaze is always hunger-filled.

"I need you to undress," Emilian says as he stands. He turns towards the linen closet behind him and rummages through it until he pulls out towels and the first aid kit, which fills me with a sense of déjà vu. "Can you manage that, or do you need my assistance?" he asks over his shoulder.

I narrow my eyes at him as he turns away, my limbs feeling heavier than before. But the last thing I fucking want is for him to think I need him for anything more than to remove this venom that is inching through my veins. If I'm going to die, it will not be at the hands of a fucking demon.

I lean forward, stifling a groan from my aching body, and attempt to shrug off my jacket. He watches me as I struggle, barely making any progress, not a hint of amusement on his face. He slowly lowers himself to his knees at my side and carefully reaches for me. I flinch as he untucks my shirt, pulling it up and exposing my abs, his knuckles brushing lightly across my skin. He doesn't take his eyes off me as he hooks a nail beneath the fabric and, with careful precision, slides it up, flaying the shirt open. He cautiously removes the soiled fabric and discards it in the trash bin that sits next to the vanity.

His hand hovers over the scars that mar my chest, as if to make sure they're still there, but he doesn't attempt to touch me. A sheen of sweat covers my body as it heats—a fever setting in as my body attempts to fight off the poison. "Where is Jax?" I ask breathlessly, leaning back and resting my head on the cabinet doors, the pain searing my lungs. "I'm surprised he didn't insist on staying."

Emilian's eyes cut up again, a ghost of a smile on his lips. "Oh, he did," he replies, his tone as smooth as a spider's silk. "But I told him that people would be more likely to question his where-abouts tonight, particularly his parents, and that he needed to lock himself up in his home and play the part of the innocent snake." He leans in slightly, forcing me to look at him as his eyes flash. "And I made a promise to him that I wouldn't eat you, no matter how badly I want to, and that seemed to settle him down."

There's a slight gleam in his eyes, his only tell that he's lying. "You used compulsion on him, didn't you?" I ask, quirking my brow, attempting to hide the smile that strings up my lips like a puppet.

Emilian shrugs, a smug smile curling at the corners of his mouth. "It's harder on beings like him, but it can be done. He might be questioning his decision to go home, but he still willingly agreed to my demands." I scoff a laugh and watch as he rummages through the first aid kit, pulling out vials marked with symbols that I've yet to identify. "Atlas, where did you get these?" Emilian asks, squinting as he lifts and examines each one, the varying liquids shimmering with an unknown magic.

"According to the note left inside, they were allegedly my mother's," I say with a sigh, attempting to close my eyes as exhaustion begins to settle into my bones, but I can't help but peek at him. "Can you hurry and just pick one? I would like to keep my fucking arm and all my other appendages."

Emilian's head snaps up with a quiet gasp, his eyes widening. "There's a book in the study that has symbols similar to these on the spine." He holds up his palm, his other hand clutching a vile. "Stay here."

"That's my *private* library," I say as I watch him rise to his feet like a cat uncurling from its midday nap. "What are you doing sneaking around in there?"

Emilian looks at me with an amused expression. "I would hardly call it sneaking around, as you've seen me in there countless times. Besides, you haven't opened a book in a decade, and you clearly haven't paid attention to the empty spaces on the shelves, or to the stack of ever-changing books on my dresser. I'd go so far as to say that I've been very open about it." He moves toward the door and glances over his shoulder. "Now, don't move, and I'll be right back."

I watch him leave, his footsteps nearly silent as he moves through the house. I close my eyes and try not to think of the thick, black veins that crawl further up my arm with every beat of my heart, threatening to consume me and possibly make me a monster. Instead, I think of Elara. Sliding my good hand into my pocket, I pull out her bracelet, the deep rubies glinting in the light. I run my thumb over the broken clasp, the metal pricking my skin, causing a small drop of blood to well up. I wipe it away, smearing the crimson on my black pants.

"Where are you, Elara?" I whisper to myself. "What are you hiding?"

Why would she have been in that section of the city alone, and where could she be now? It will only be a matter of time before we are called out to complete a mission, and I don't know if I'll be able to protect her once they realize that she hasn't been with me this entire time. I can only pretend she reported for the mission and stave off Brander and Ransley for so long, and they would definitely have questions if she wasn't with me when we reported in.

I could always claim her to be ill or injured, but it wouldn't take long for them to go to her apartment looking for her, and then I would be in a world of trouble. It was smart of Emilian to compel Jax to go home and keep him out of this as much as possible. Jax will protect Elara just as much as I will, but at some point, we'll have to decide between her and ourselves.

But right now, I just want to know if she's even alive.

I clutch her bracelet in my hand, pressing my fingertips into the jewels, and think back through the past few weeks, wondering if there were any signs that my dumbass missed. I huff out a sigh, bumping my already-throbbing head against the vanity door, as if I can tap into my brain.

She went dark after our Roundtable meeting, where it was not lost on me that the Knight—the shifter—sitting next to her was watching her as if she was intended to be his next meal. Who is he, and why was he so enamored with her that night?

Did he follow her home and kidnap her? Did she run off with him?

I don't remember seeing his Legion signet, but to be honest, I wasn't necessarily paying attention; he gave off the same vibes as most of the shifters that he's not to be fucked with. It's also entirely possible that I'm just pointing fingers at a being who was overly aware of the tension between Elara and me and was just doing his duty to ensure that everything remained calm, especially during a Roundtable. Things can occasionally become heated when such powerful beings are all present in one room and there has been more than the fair share of brawls break out.

I'll note him at the next meeting, and if I haven't found Elara by then, maybe he can provide me with some answers. To what, exactly? I don't know. But I'm so desperate that I'll accept anything that might lead me in the right direction. I just need to keep believing that she's still in the city and not lost in another realm.

Emilian walks back in, absentmindedly flipping through the pages of a book, murmuring to himself. He stops suddenly, the heels of his shoes squeaking on the floor. He takes a deep inhale through his nose, his pupils widening as his gaze cuts to me. "You're bleeding," he says roughly.

I look down at my thumb where the blood still gathers, threatening to drip down my hand. "I cut it on Elara's bracelet," I say casually, still staring at the crimson bubble. "It's nothing."

I see a movement out of the corner of my eye, but before I can react, Emilian is on me, his hand wrapping around mine, forcing my thumb back. The whites of his eyes are framed in black, and I gently try to pull my hand away, but his vise-like grip holds me in place.

"Emilian," I say calmly. "Please, let me go." I want to jerk my hand away, plant my boot in the middle of his chest, and kick him back, but I'm frozen in place.

His gaze turns distant, as if he's lost in a trance. The book in his other hand drops to the floor, face up, with the page fully displayed. "Just one taste," he murmurs. "That's all I need." Everything about him becomes sharper, from the line of his jaw to his elongating fangs, morphing into the monster that we both work hard to keep locked away.

Elara used to warn me that it would be the smallest thing that would make him turn on me, but who knew that it would be something of hers that would end up being the cause of my demise?

I slide my free hand back into my pocket, but the stake that used to be there is now nothing more than black tar in the street from where it was lodged in the demon's skull. *Shit.* I'm injured and utterly defenseless against a being who could rip me apart limb by limb or drain me dry. I yank my hand, but still, he doesn't let it go.

"I will let you feed tonight, Emilian." My voice wavers, giving away the fear that's sinking its deadly claws into my chest and curling around my heart.

"*Just. One. Taste.*" His words are as sharp as his fangs, his own blood dripping from his lips where the needle-like tips have pricked them and threaten to tear away his skin. He raises my hand to his mouth, his breath warm against my skin as his tongue flicks out, catching the single drop of blood just as it cascades down my thumb.

He groans, the sound vibrating between us, causing a curl of heat in my abdomen. His long tongue wraps around my thumb, cleaning off any remnants of blood, as his eyes cut to the gaping, oozing wound on my arm. Still clutching my hand, he raises his free one to his mouth, piercing the skin at his wrist as if he's biting into an apple. Even with his wild eyes, he's eerily calm as he raises his arm to my mouth, the blood dripping to the floor. "Drink," he says roughly. His whole demeanor changes rapidly, like a dark storm forming on the horizon.

"Emilian, I—"

"*Drink,*" he growls as he shoves his wrist to my mouth, pressing it against my lips, the metallic taste of his blood seeping onto my tongue. I hesitate, but slowly part my lips and press them tightly against his wrist, his musky scent filling my nose as I swipe my tongue over his decadent skin. I take a long pull, mimicking his movements from when he feeds on me, the warmth flowing effortlessly down my throat.

"Just like that," he says, his voice almost a purr. "Now, keep your eyes on me. I'll tell you when to stop."

My arm tingles, but I don't dare look down; I keep my gaze on him as I take another long pull. I want to fight this feeling, push back and resist his commands, but there's a voice that calls from a dark corner of my mind, growing louder as it encourages me to keep going—to take from him like I've let him take from me for all these years.

So, I do.

I turn my long pulls into short, rough sucks, pulling his skin taunt. His red irises heat as the onyx edges begin to take over, his desire imminent as they nearly roll back in his head. He releases my hand and places his on the vanity beside my head, his body leaning forward as he begins to close the space between us. I reach up and grip his wrist, my core thrumming so hard it becomes painful, but I don't stop. My body heats, making me feel as if he's feeding on me, throwing me into a euphoric state and craving more.

More blood.

More of him.

I glide my hand up his arm and across his neck, looping my finger through the ring of his collar and pulling him in even closer. His lips curl into a near-feral smile as I stare deeply into his eyes. I keep waiting for my mind to turn fuzzy and my vision to become cloudy, but everything remains crystal clear.

I'm more than aware of how fucked up this is, but I can't seem to stop—and I don't want to.

"Then don't," Emilian says roughly, his nostrils flaring as he breathes deeply. "Take all you need from me. Take *everything*. Drink me dry if that's what you want—what you *need*."

My cock twitches, throbbing as I take another deep pull. His blood is sweet, like my favorite wine, and tastes nothing like I thought it would. Emilian's eyes roll back in his head as a groan escapes his lips. His hips buck against me as his warmth fills me. He takes a deep, shuddering breath before he slowly pulls his wrist away, my lips pursing as I try desperately to keep them pressed against his skin, until it's finally out of reach.

Our breaths are erratic, filling the space between us with desperation. I watch as his eyes flicker down to where my arm rests at my side, and I follow his gaze. I raise it, and gasp at the sight of my smooth skin. The wounds have closed, and the black veins have vanished without a trace, not even a scar from the demon's jagged teeth remains. My eyes widen as I glance back up at Emilian, the corners of his mouth curling into a sly smile. "Just as I always suspected."

II

ATLAS

I POUR ANOTHER FINGER OF SCOTCH AND THROW IT BACK BEFORE I'M once again pacing through the study, my mind racing. What does this fucking mean? I knew vampires had healing powers; that's how Emilian healed me all those years ago, but that took a few days, and it left an obvious scar that I have kept tucked away.

But this? It doesn't make any sense.

I stand shirtless, staring into the fire as it burns brightly, licking at the edges of the hearth. I mindlessly rub my hand over the rough edges of my scar while staring down at the now-healed skin on my arm, where it's extended, my hand gripping the carved mantle. I listen as Emilian flips through the pages of an old book, one that bears my mother's handwritten name in the front, with most of the text inside in her delicate handwriting.

"The symbol you carved on me that night," I start, not looking away from the flames. "What does it *actually* mean? And don't fucking twist your words."

Emilian turns another page, letting the silence hang between us, compelling me to turn toward him. He's watching me from across the room, the flickering flames casting shadows across his face, enhancing the sharp line of his jaw. "Balance."

My eyes narrow. "I thought it was supposed to be a symbol of protection?" I ask, my face heating from more than the fire that roars next to me. "You promised me *protection*."

"And I gave it to you," he says lowly, looking down his nose at me. "You would not be here without me."

My face flushes even hotter as I cross my arms, my fingers curling into fists, pressing against my biceps. "You don't have the power here." My teeth are gritted, the words spilling through the spaces between them. "*I do*."

"Because you are a Knight?" he asks, snapping the book shut in his hand, letting out a dark laugh. "You are nothing more than a mere human mortal. An orphan who would have never had the chance to become a Knight of the Vail if it hadn't been for me. You call *me* the pet, but who's the one begging all the time? Who's the one really on a leash?"

My rage ignites, an internal flame that makes me see red. I reach for the sword that hangs above the fireplace, the metal ringing as I drag it down. I grip it in both hands and step toward him.

I will fucking *kill* him and end this infernal game of cat and mouse once and for all.

"Do it, then," he growls. "*End it*."

I stare at him, my jaw slackening. Did I say that out loud? No, I know I didn't, but how could he have heard me?

His eyes widen, and I feel a slight pull in my chest as if an anchor has hooked into me, ready to toss me over the edge of this inevitably sinking ship, threatening to drag me under. But I ignore it—instead, I take another step toward him, raising the blade higher. His eyes stay on mine, not backing down as he squares his shoulders. "You know what you are, Atlas." His eyes flare.

"A *Knight*," I bite out, swinging the blade, letting it slice through the tension that's rising between us. "A Knight of the

Vail." I thrust the blade out as I take another step, the tip pressing against his throat. "And your fucking *sire*."

He keeps his eyes on me, his pupils widening until his red irises are nothing more than a thin ring, his body still as stone. "This book," he says, lifting it to eye level, "says you are more. It's been here, ready to tell you everything you've ever wanted to know about your family, about who you really are. If you'd only taken the time to look."

"I have no real family," I bite out, my arms trembling at the weight that pushes down on them. "The Knighthood is my family now."

It's technically a lie, I know. Everyone has a family some-where, whether they're still breathing, six feet under, or nothing more than dust in the wind.

But I was left alone.

Forfeited.

I am nothing more than an orphan to the city I have vowed my life to protect.

I inherited this house on my eighteenth birthday when a parcel was anonymously delivered to the orphanage. It lay on the stoop, collected by the Headmaster, Gabriel, and delivered straight to me. Yellowed with time, the edges were grayed with dust and debris from wherever it had once been stored. Inside was a handwritten note and a single brass key.

The note was brief, written in a delicate script, stating that I was the proud owner of a three-story townhouse, along with everything in it, and I was to keep it safe from the evils of the world. I took that as a sign that I was destined to be a Knight, that I was being given my first test, and if I failed, then I would lose everything. Little did I know that I would one day invite a vampire into my life, into my home, and defy the one request that my family made of me.

I was delivered to the townhouse immediately that evening, per the note's instructions, with the Headmaster as my only escort. Elara begged to come with us, desperately wanting to leave the grounds and join me in the start of my new life. I remember her fingers wrapped tightly around the metal bars of the gate, her eyes glassy with tears as we disappeared into the twilight, leaving my old life and Elara behind, for now.

The Headmaster followed me up the stairs but didn't dare pass the threshold, his body stiff even from where he stood on the stoop. Standing in the foyer, key clutched in my hand, ready to ask him to follow me in, he simply held his hand up to silence me. He bid farewell and reminded me that I was still expected to be at my regular training at sunrise. I watched as he slipped into the shadows of the darkening streets, and as far as I know, he has yet to leave the orphanage grounds again.

Emilian clears his throat, bringing my attention back to him, as he rolls his eyes. "If you have no family, then how do you explain the fact of your mysterious inheritance? Not to mention, no one at the orphanage questioned how you ended up with all of this?" He gestures around the study, the bookshelves packed from floor to ceiling with books that I haven't bothered to crack open.

Meanwhile, Emilian has been reading them for almost a decade. "I have fought against every instinct that was cursed upon me and learned how to behave in this house, because even though I was invited in, what do you think would happen to me if I misbehaved? The spirits of the past are unforgiving to the undead. Why do you think there was already a cell in the basement, Atlas?"

I stare at him as his voice grows sharper with every word—a blade gliding across a whetstone, as if he is preparing to have his own sword at *my* throat. "For their enemies," I say quietly, the words turning sour on my tongue as more realization of my lineage slams into me. The covens that once lived in the city were powerful, but with that power came targets on their backs —other beings ready to destroy those who could wield magic of all kinds.

Emilian leans into the blade of the sword, letting the tip of it press roughly into his skin, but not enough to break it. "For *your* enemies, Atlas," he retorts. "For monsters like *me*."

I lower the blade, the sharp tip accidentally nicking his skin, letting loose a small trickle of blood before it swiftly heals, leaving behind nothing more than a line of crimson across his moonlight skin. "You're not my enemy, Emilian." I look down at my exposed chest and take in the symbol that was lightly carved into it—that *he* carved on that faithful night.

"*Aren't I?*" His eyes narrow. "I have always been the bane of your existence, have I not? I am nothing more than your little burden of a pet. The one that you wish to put down and be rid of for good."

"That's not true," I start, but he keeps going, barely taking a breath.

"Haven't you said that I'm nothing more than a parasite? A fucking *vermin*? Or has that all been a lie? Just like the string of them you let pile up for the last decade that are now threatening to collapse on top of us."

"Emilian—"

He holds up a hand, turning and picking up the muzzle that lay on the desk behind him. "Put this back on me. I am ready to retire to my dwelling and let you be."

I swallow thickly as my heart thunders in my chest. I stare at the muzzle, the sight of it sending a punch to my gut and I shake my head. "You don't need—"

He steps toward me, putting the muzzle directly in front of my face. "I know the rules, *sire*," he bites out, the word like a hard slap, nearly making me stumble back as he snaps his teeth dangerously close to my throat, ready to tear it open.

My fingers curl around the muzzle, and I let the weight of it hang in my hand. I watch him, waiting for his sharp, red irises to soften like they normally would when we get into tiffs, but he simply juts out his chin. His gaze slices through me, adding an invisible mark to my scarred chest, attempting to pierce my heart.

I press it to his face, pulling the straps behind his head to the base of his skull, my hands getting lost in his black curtain of hair. I breathe in his musky scent and look into his eyes, never breaking my gaze as I loop the strap through the buckle, tightening it just enough to hold it in place, but not to be uncomfortable. I hesitate; the urge to grip his nape and keep him in place is unbearable. However, he steps away, and as he does, my fingers slide through his hair, the tips aching.

He steps widely around me as he exits the room and fades into the shadows that shroud the hall in darkness. The incessant tug in my chest urges me to follow him, and even as it threatens to steal my breath, I remain rooted in place. I was trained to trust my instincts and follow my target in any direction, but right now, I need to let him have time to cool off, even as the scar on my chest tingles and a deep ache settles into my chest.

I look down at my arm and run my fingers over the smooth skin, the gruesome image of what it looked like before forever burned into my mind. Another reminder of what the creatures of Hell are capable of. I round the massive desk and sit down in the tufted leather chair, the wooden wheels creaking as I roll it forward. Sliding the book that Emilian left toward me, I flip through it, looking for the last page he had been on, but instead, I spot the exact symbol that is carved into my chest. I run my fingers over the light scar, tracing its outline.

Balance.

Emilian saved my life that night nearly ten years ago. He carved the symbol delicately into my skin after I was fully healed, and even as his eyes were heated with hunger, I never once felt threatened by him—not even as the blood trickled down my chest. The pain was minuscule in comparison to the gaping hole that the demon had left. The bargain we made was for him to become what we would consider my pet, a willing assistant to the Knighthood. Unless he were out on a mission, he would only be allowed to dwell in my home and feed under my watchful eye.

I planned to protect him from immediate death or being ruthlessly shoved through an open rift, thrown into whatever Hellish dimension was waiting on the other side. Emilian at my back gave me power over my peers, the illusion that I had captured and tamed a vicious vampire—all of it no more than a show filled with smoke and mirrors.

He's the true hero, not me.

To everyone, I'm a Knight of Vail, but I don't know who or what the hell I am anymore. Even as I took a vow to the city and proudly wear the crest as a badge of honor, the scar on my chest tells the whole story—that I'm weak.

If fate had its way that night, I would have never become a Knight, and more than likely wouldn't even be alive anymore. I cheated on the most crucial test of my life, and that's why it's so important to keep everything hidden away.

To keep *him* hidden away.

No matter how I spin it, no matter how hard I try to ignore it, I'm nothing short of a fraud in every sense of the word. I've always said that I wanted to be free of Emilian, but it's obvious he would be far better off without me, in this life and any after.

12

EMILIAN

THE BASS FROM THE MUSIC ON THE FIRST FLOOR THUMPS THROUGH the house, occasionally causing dust to loosen and float down from the rafters. It catches the dim light of the lamp on the side table next to my bed, resembling falling snow as it lands on the surfaces below. I adjust the chain linking my collar to the anchor bolted to the wall, the metal clinking softly together, as my fingers play with the clip that I could easily undo.

Atlas is hosting a party with his Knightly friends as they gather to celebrate another year of his life in this dark and decaying city that he proudly calls home. It's late—well past midnight—and approaching the witching hour. Although the music is still blaring from the speakers, I sense the party is winding down, with only a handful of people remaining compared to the dozens who arrived at the start of the night.

I can only imagine how tightly wound they are, their Chancellors constantly breathing down their necks and sending them out to patrol the streets as more and more monsters step through the rifts. Atlas has proudly risen through the ranks and is barely home as he works on his own missions and trains incoming Knights, preparing them for their initiations.

I've continuously told him to lie low, do what is necessary, and stay back in the shadows. The less attention he draws to himself, the easier it will all be in the end. But as a mortal man, he feels he has much to prove to the company and their Grand Master. I audibly groan at the thought of him licking the boots of any of those Chancellors while he's on his knees, giving himself over to them as if he owes them his life, while simultaneously being fucked over.

The house quiets as someone lowers the volume, and I sigh in relief, removing the earplugs I grabbed from a junk drawer in the kitchen in preparation for his party. Atlas is known to get rowdy with his colleagues, and even an undead being like myself can be driven to madness by their music choices. The uninterrupted silence allows me to catch up on the reading I've been putting off and to stare into the abyss, delving deep into the thoughts that plague my sleepless mind.

I've found through the years that the study's library has a fascinating collection of books, ranging from old textbooks to classic novels, bodice rippers, and the occasional grimoire from an unnamed coven. Over the years, I've slowly been cataloging and organizing them according to the Dewey Decimal System, and Atlas has never seemed to notice. In fact, I doubt he's been in the study more than a dozen times during my years of living here.

Atlas is knowledgeable, but it's evident that studying bores him, as he lives for the action, the glory, and the thrill of his endless missions. He certainly doesn't experience the same excitement by sitting down with a book and learning about the past or another's life outside of the Knights he was partying with tonight. Even then, they only know each other for their accomplishments within the Vail and the parts of themselves they want to show, keeping the rest hidden.

For instance, I doubt they know Atlas drinks his coffee black when others are around, but he enjoys a creamy, frothy latte behind closed doors, letting the foam collect on his upper lip. He also hums in the shower, making up his own tunes, and stays in there until the hot water turns ice cold. Not to mention, he pretends to like scotch in front of company, but genuinely enjoys sparkling red wine and can finish the entire bottle in one sitting.

They call themselves comrades, but that's only half the truth. I've seen the parts of him that he hides from the world, the ones that he shoves into the basement alongside me, never to see the light of day. And they're as rare as a valuable gem, one I'm not willing to share with anyone else.

Time ticks by as I reread one of my favorite poetry collections for the umpteenth time and find myself wishing that someday I could return to my old home, which is undoubtedly condemned or destroyed by now, and collect the books I cherished so deeply. However, that would mean being allowed to leave the premises without being on a mission, which would break the rules of the bargain I made with Atlas and the terms the Grand Master added to keep me in an eternal lockdown.

Fuck their Grand Master and all their ridiculous rules.

To them, I would be nothing more than a rabid dog needing to be put down for the good of the city, or so they'd say, and they would find even the smallest reason to have me destroyed. And while Atlas claims to loathe my existence, I do not doubt that he would escort me to my old home, on the other side of the city, and allow me to retrieve whatever is left. But then I would have to face the life that was ripped from me, left in nothing but a pile of rubble to decay with time, and my undead heart is full of enough cracks that I fear that might finally break it.

I hear the thud of footsteps reverberate through the house, stopping momentarily in the foyer. Quiet laughs and murmurs fill the air before they're silenced. The door clicks closed, and the locks are secured, sealing us inside.

I listen intently for any additional footfalls of an unexpected overnight guest, but I only hear the soft thud of Atlas's feet as they pad through the house. I catch the quiet clink of bottles as he gathers them up in the kitchen and the soft thunk as they land in the garbage can.

Atlas is what you consider a bachelor, but he certainly doesn't live like one. He keeps the house neat; his laundry is always washed and folded the same day, and there's hardly a smudge on any surface. The only dark, dirty mark in this house, or on him, is me.

I settle back against my pillow, resting my book on the crook of my leg, and listen to him as he moves around the house, going through his nightly routine. However, this time, his footsteps halt at the basement door, where he stands unmoving for a long moment. I close my eyes and listen closely, the quiet thud of his racing heart pulsing through the floorboards, pushing his sweet blood through his veins.

The bolt slides free, the basement door opens with a quiet creak as he carefully steps down onto the first step. The pungent scent of alcohol filters through the air, and if he makes it down the stairs in one piece, it will be nothing less than a fucking miracle. Flickering my gaze up, I watch as he stumbles off the last step, his fingers curling around the bars of my enclosure, the metal rattling. He quietly hiccups as he slides the key into the lock, the barred door swinging open.

He crosses the room cautiously, as if he's just stepped into the cage of a dangerous animal...and tonight, maybe he has. Sitting up, I turn and let my legs fall over the edge of the bed, my bare feet pressing into the large, plush antique area rug that fills most of the space. I don't say anything as he comes closer, his pupils wide from behind his alcohol-heavy lids.

He stops in front of me and loops his finger through the O-ring of my collar, where I don't resist as he brings me to my feet. "Atlas," I say in a tone that borders on warning. Still, he acts as though he doesn't hear, his fingers weaving through my hair until they meet the buckle at the base of my skull, his nimble fingers only slightly stumbling as he undoes my muzzle. It falls from my face, bouncing across the floor as he watches me, his eyes flickering down to my lips as he licks his own.

His gaze is intense, with his breaths shallow and somewhat

erratic. The tension between us is almost palpable, and I feel a gentle tug in my chest, drawing me closer to him. His hands glide down my exposed chest, tracing the muscles of my abdomen before landing on the laces of my pants. He pauses, glancing from my already-hardening cock to my widening pupils. The scent of his arousal fills my nostrils, causing my mouth to water. I don't even have to look to see he's already hard, precum leaking from the tip, and begging for a release that he denies himself for far too long.

"On your knees," he says breathlessly, his fingers still tracing the waistband of my pants. "And hands behind your back."

I give him a sly smile as I sink to my knees, his fingers brushing up my body, and clasp my hands behind my back as he commands. Our relationship is more than unconventional, but we seem to make it work. I love to submit to his demands, regardless of their nature, and he enjoys the thrill of thinking he's the one in charge, all while I reap the benefits. It's regrettable that he only becomes this brave and demanding when he's been drinking and his testosterone is pumping hot through him, making him something, if not feral.

He slowly unfastens his jeans, showing a casual style with his plain white shirt, which the outside world rarely sees. They fall to his bare feet, and he steps out of them, kicking them away. His fingers grasp the waistband of his boxers; his bulge already prominent, and I note the slight wet spot that's formed on the fabric—the sight making my fangs elongate. He lets them fall to the floor, nudging them to the side, before gripping the hem of the shirt and shucking it off, where it lands beside him.

I look him over, my hungry gaze taking in every bulging muscle, as he stands wholly naked before me, his chiseled body like that of a marble statue. He's grown into his body, showing that his hard work and countless hours working out are paying off. His broad chest rises and falls with every breath, spanning out to the corded muscles of his arms, the veins pressing against his skin. His lean waist meets at a V, bringing my eyes down to his most valuable asset. I lick my lips at his thick cock with a delicious, pulsing vein that runs up the underside, standing at attention, begging me to have a taste.

"I'm going to fuck your mouth, *pet*," he says heavily, a growl forming deep in his chest, the cocktail of alcohol and lust slowing down his thoughts. "You'll swallow my cum like you do my blood and take every last drop. Drink me dry."

My cock twitches as he stares down at me, stroking his length, coating it with his desire. He steps closer, running his free hand through my hair, gripping the strands roughly, and pulling me closer. Flicking my tongue out, I lick away the dripping precum, the taste of him blooming in my mouth.

A sinful taste of heaven in this forbidden hellscape.

He groans as I unclasp my hands from behind me, defying him in every way I possibly can and begging for punishment. I graze my palms up the backs of his thighs, lightly scraping my nails against the sensitive skin, leaving delicate red lines in their wake. Gripping his ass, I guide him into my mouth, swirling my tongue over his shaft and taking him all the way to the hilt. His grip tightens in my hair as he starts to move his hips with small thrusts, like the staccato notes of the grandest symphony.

I let out a deep moan, allowing it to resonate through both of us and shake the ground. Atlas is lost in ecstasy as he grips the collar at my throat, my nails transforming into sharp claws that prick his skin, warmth welling across my fingertips. The sweet smell of his blood fills the air as he hisses through his teeth.

"Emilian," he moans. "Oh, *fuck*."

I pull back, his cock popping free from my lips as I bring a hand around, gripping his balls and running my tongue along the underside of his shaft. He widens his stance as my hands and mouth roam freely across his skin. My fangs elongate more, and I gently scrape them across his inner thigh, eliciting another guttural moan from him and unraveling him stitch by stitch.

His grip tightens, and he wrenches my head back, forcing my gaze up to him. "Did I say you could use your teeth?" he growls, his tone causing a sharp tingle to pulse up my spine, heat spreading through me.

I smirk, letting my fangs shine in the low light. "I didn't ask," I quip, slowly scraping my claws down the back of his thigh, my other hand gripping his cock, his heat dripping onto my bare chest. His scent is intoxicating, making me lightheaded as I become drunk on the power this game gives me. I'm pushing my limits tonight, and it's a foolish game, but always one worth playing. He's at odds with himself, and I love seeing the fight he puts up in a battle he's always been destined to lose.

The number of times he's come stumbling down here for more than just to let me feed is more than he'd ever admit. However, I never miss the scent of his release as he comes, safe and warm in his own bed, into his own hand, especially when tensions arise between us. His muscles are corded and dense, but he's nothing more than a delicate human.

Breakable.

I run my tongue up his inner thigh, hovering my fangs over the large vein that pulses and presses against his skin. With a glance, I meet his heated gaze, the gleam in his eyes begging me to take just one bite—and I love when he begs. Without hesitation, I pierce his skin, his delicious blood filling my mouth as I pump my hand up and down his length, his hands roughly gripping my hair to hold himself steady, his knees threatening to buckle. His guttural moan sends my own throbbing cock over the edge, the heat of my own seed warming between my legs, dripping onto the floor through the fabric of my pants.

I get lost in my own desire, and I don't know how long it's been as his blood fills me, making me hard all over again. "Emilian," he gasps, *"please."* His voice pulls me back, and I pull my mouth away, his blood dripping down my chin, licking it from my lips.

His shallow breaths fall between us as blood trickles down his leg. I glide my tongue over the red rivulets, collecting them on my tongue. I open my mouth wide, his length filling the space, and he fucks my face. He seizes the control he so desperately needs as his blood covers my chin and chest, never taking his eyes off me.

I rest my hands on my thighs and watch as he slips a hand from my scalp and up to his nipple, pinching it roughly until a bruise begins to form. Atlas loves the pain. His body craves it in every way, always trying to find release where he can, proving that he's a raging masochist. He's had partners through the years, but none seem to satisfy him the way I do with my fangs and claws.

It's not long before his rhythm stutters as his hot cum mixes with my saliva and his blood as it pours down my throat, a growl tearing from him as he slams into my mouth one last time. His hand slides out of my hair as he looks down at me, and for what I believe is the first time, there doesn't seem to be a flicker of shame in his gaze. I lick my lips, a satisfied grin tugging at the corners of my mouth as I run my hands carefully up his thighs.

"Atlas," I say with a purr, letting the warmth of his name course through me, sending me on another wave of pleasure. "Tell me what you want from me."

I don't believe in the gods, new or old, as they've failed me time and time again, but I can't help but fall to my knees at his altar. I'll say his name like a pleading prayer until it's my time to walk into the bowels of Hell, delivering him the stake that he will undoubtedly drive into my heart, ending my pathetic existence once and for all.

He holds my gaze, and I watch in horror as his eyes shift, causing everything to come crashing down. He takes in the scene before him, with the mix of blood, cum, and...*me*. He stumbles back, his lip curling into a silent snarl. And where his eyes are usually wide and filled with panic, this time, they darken with sheer disgust.

Absolute disdain.

He reaches down and grabs his clothes, his blood-covered hand staining the bleach-white shirt, soiling it. As he sobers, the alcohol and lust clearing from his vision, he looks at me as if I had lured him into my web and attempted to eat him alive. That I truly am nothing more than a pest...*vermin*...that has infested his life.

"Atlas." His name is just a choking sound as it tries to lodge in my throat, its barbs ripping into me. The anchor in my chest grows heavier with each step he takes backward, pulling it down into the dark abyss, the pressure causing more fissures to appear across my heart. "*Please.*"

He shakes his head, his eyes turning, flashing with rage as his neck and face become flushed. "Stay the fuck away from me, you fucking *monster.*" The word snaps at me like a hellhound. He spins and strides out of the cell, slamming the door and wrenching the key as the lock bolts into place. He fists the key tightly in his hands and hauls himself up the stairs.

The dust from the floor joists floats around me as he stomps through the house, settling on me, not like snow, but like ash, as the last remnants of my world go up in flames. I watch as they transform into nothing more than glowing embers, snuffing out like my dead, shattered heart.

13

ATLAS

A COLD WIND WHIPS AROUND ME AS THE SETTING SUN DISAPPEARS behind the rooftops, piercing my skin like talons as I stalk through the streets, scanning the shadows for any movement. Jax checks all the windows of the rundown buildings, as our search for Elara seems likely to continue well into the night.

"Tell me again why you didn't bring your little pet along this time?" Jax asks from his position on the fire escape ladder that stretches up from the dark alley he's led us into, his boot squeaking quietly against the rung as he shifts to look down at me.

I shrug, keeping my face neutral even as my cheeks heat, the cold already making them look flushed. "Like I said, I think he might have attracted the demon with his vampire scent. I want to make sure that it doesn't happen again and jeopardize our investigation."

Lies, lies, lies.

If a monster wanted to, it could rip open the veil right in front of us, Emilian present or not, and tear us limb from limb.

Jax watches me closely, his serpent eyes narrowing to slits as he looks down at my arm. "How's your arm, anyway?" he asks, a wariness in his tone. "It looks as though the venom didn't kill you or eat away at your brain."

I raise my arm, hidden away by a wrapped bandage, concealing my perfectly healed skin. "It's healing," I say casually. "And for once, you were right, I did need to seek *actual* medical care," I say with a laugh, the lie coming out far too easily. And just like I'd hoped, his sharp eyes soften, and he lets out his own chuckle, all the doubt he had falling away.

"That was some really fucked up shit," Jax says as he climbs the ladder further up the fire escape, the metal balcony creaking under his weight as he shifts to investigate a cracked window. "What kind of demon was that anyway? I've never seen anything like it."

The image of the monster flashes through my mind, sending a shiver up my spine. "I don't know, but they've only been getting worse in this area," I reply. "Makes you wonder what fucking circle of Hell, or other realm, it came from." I pull myself up the ladder behind him as he continues up to the roof of the building.

The cold from the metal bites into my exposed fingertips as I continue up from the landing to the rooftop, where the wind is even more vicious as it blows wildly around us. I halt my steps, catching movement out of the corner of my eye. I turn and see that someone is on another fire escape a few streets over, their long, dark hair whipping around in the wind. "Someone's over there," I say, the wind carrying my voice to Jax. The thought of Emilian following me since I never went down to lock his cell crosses my mind, but I squash it like a bug—he knows better than to leave the house without me and risk himself being caught alone.

Jax looks over his shoulder at me, following my line of sight. "Just another Knight, I'm sure," he says with a shrug. "And even if it's not, that's not what we're here for tonight, right?"

I nod and give him a quiet grunt in reply. I watch them for a few blinks and see that it's a woman in a dark jacket, her back to us as she scans the street below. It's clear we're not her target for the evening, and I finally let loose a breath and relax my shoulders before turning my attention back to Jax, where he stands at the edge of the roof, ready to leap to the other side.

"What are we doing up here anyway?" I ask as we move from one side of the rooftop to the other, jumping between the buildings like feral alley cats.

His body shifts, his scales shimmering in the last of the daylight as it peeks over the horizon. "I thought this would give us a better view of the street and *not* be bombarded by another demon. I don't know if we'd be so lucky this time, and as much as I hate to admit it, your little leech saved our asses."

I quirk a brow. Even though he tries to drip disdain into his words, they come up flat, almost as if he truly appreciates Emilian being around last night. But I don't press him and just give a knowing nod instead. He's right about the fact that this does give us a better view, but if a demon sensed us, we would go from being the hunter to the hunted in a single breath.

I give him a cocky smile, trying to keep the mood as light as possible. "He does live under my roof, so I'm sure he's picked up a thing or two," I say with a wink. "I am, in fact, a medaled Knight, you know?"

Jax rolls his eyes, letting out a quiet scoff as we continue across the rooftops. The only sound is the roar of the wild wind, blocking any noise from below. The sun winks out behind the skyscrapers, cloaking us in darkness and making us invisible to the rest of the city in our dark clothing. Jax pauses, looking down at the space between his feet. "Someone's in here," he says lowly.

"How many?" I ask, staying still.

He cocks his head to the side, his brows knitting together. "It looks like only one, but we can't be too sure."

We approach the edge of the building, Jax swinging his leg over and carefully descending the fire escape. I watch as he eases his way down, the ladder shaking with every step, looking as though it's threatening to slip right off the side of the building and crash to the ground.

"Are you coming or not?" he snaps, his whisper floating up along the brick from where he hangs almost halfway down. I huff a breath and follow his lead. I carefully swing my leg over the side, bracing my boot on one of the rungs, the metal creaking under my added weight.

I take a deep breath and slowly descend the ladder, feeling it shake with every step. I examine the bolts I pass, anxiety prickling at the back of my neck in anticipation of the whole thing giving out and dropping me to my death. But by a stroke of luck, we both manage to set our feet on the solid ground beneath, and I let loose a jagged breath.

Jax looks down at his feet, his head cocking to the side again as he slowly turns in a circle, his brows stitching together. I follow his gaze as a slight tremor shakes up my legs, causing his head to snap up, his eyes wide with panic. "Atlas—"

I turn to Jax just as another tremor rumbles beneath our feet so violently that it throws us off balance, sending us both stumbling as Jax falls backward, his body splayed out on the ground. I reach out my hand as I step forward to help him, my foot never landing back on the ground as it falls out from beneath me. A scream lodges in my throat as my arms catch me on the edge of the giant hole that opened around me, clawing at the crumbling alley floor.

"Jax!" I cry out; his name comes out choked as the lump of panic in my throat grows larger. My legs scramble from where they hang in midair, trying to plant themselves on anything to hoist myself up. Only, there's nothing but darkness.

Adrenaline pulses through me as my nails scrape and crack along the asphalt. I squeeze my eyes closed as the image of a demon grabbing my ankles and wrenching me down fills my mind's eye. My shoulders scream in pain as I try to pull myself out, chunks of asphalt falling into the pit, getting lost in the abyss.

"*Atlas,*" Jax yells as he rolls back in my direction, panic filling his eyes as he scrambles to his feet. His rough hands curl around my wrists, gripping me tightly as he begins to hoist me up. "Hang on."

The jagged edges of the hole scrape across my abdomen, threatening to tear me open as Jax continues to drag me away, his hisses filling the air. He keeps going until we're completely clear of the hole before he drops my wrists. I roll onto my back and stare at where Jax now stands over me, bent in half with his hands on his knees, both of us gasping for air.

I lift myself on my elbows, waiting for the hole to widen its mouth, ready to swallow up its next victim. After a few moments of silence, the dust around the edges finally settles, with only shadows inside shifting in the wind.

"What the fuck just happened?" Jax asks breathlessly, looking over me at the hole that's about seven feet wide, the loose edges continuing to crumble as debris falls into oblivion. "I've never seen the ground open like that, and nothing came out." He stretches to investigate, concern etched onto his face. "Unless something is waiting down there."

We've seen and heard about some crazy shit through the years, but this is like no other rift I've ever seen. It looks like a normal sinkhole that has occasionally appeared around the city, causing a wave of panic, only to be quickly debunked and filled back in. There were always signs of a cave-in, like fissures and dips in the street, but this was too sudden and happened on what had been claimed to be solid ground. And unlike other rifts we've encountered, nothing has stepped through this one, not to mention that it hasn't closed back up, almost as if it's nothing more than a decoy.

"Let's get the fuck out of here," I say as I get to my feet, dusting myself off, pebbles clattering to the ground. "We'll call in an anonymous tip, and someone else can fucking deal with this."

"Can we *do* that?" Jax asks as I step around him and off the sidewalk back onto the street. "I thought that as Knights we were supposed to handle this kind of thing? Block off the area and make sure no one gets hurt."

I cut him a look. "Do you want to explain to the Chancellors what exactly we're doing out here?" His cheeks redden as he runs his hand over his head, his lips pressing into a thin line. "We're not on an official mission, Jax, and it will make us look extremely suspicious if we're here with a gaping hole in the ground and no demon to show for it. Plus, we don't have any information on Elara's whereabouts. They expect me to be with her, not you, and the last thing I want is for her to be exiled over something stupid like this."

He continues to run his hand over his head, his fingers digging into the short curls as he groans. "You're right. I'm sorry. I'm just so fucking worried about her, man." He looks around at the abandoned street and back to the townhouse, the sinkhole lost in the shadows of the alley. "And something's just not right. The air is wrong out here."

I take a step toward the stoop, and out of the corner of my eye, I see a flutter of movement in one of the front windows. I keep my face straight ahead, my gaze sidelong, watching as the curtains fall back together, as if someone had just parted them.

"Jax," I say quietly, but his eyes are already fixed on the window, watching like the powerful predator that lies in wait beneath his skin.

"Someone's still in there," he mutters, taking a step forward, but I throw out my arm, stopping him.

His brows climb up his forehead as I point back down the alley, curling my finger as if I'm pointing directly at the back of the house. He nods, and we turn and slowly move to the back door of the house. We press ourselves against the brick, careful not to get too close to the sinkhole that is widening more with each passing second, sharpening its teeth, ready to swallow us straight to Hell.

That is, if whoever is inside doesn't get to us first.

14

ATLAS

"THIS WAS ALMOST TOO EASY," JAX WHISPERS FROM BEHIND ME AS the back door quietly creaks open to a seemingly vacant kitchen.

I step in, pulling my gun from the holster in my waistband, and sweep the kitchen. "Do you see anything?" I ask, looking up at the ceiling as if I possess the same abilities as this Basilisk.

He brushes past me and slowly looks around, searching for the source of heat from the person we caught in the window. He slowly approaches a doorway, peeking his head through as he makes his way to the front of the house. I keep my distance to let him work, but cover him as he leads the way. "Someone was definitely here." He narrows his gaze as he looks over his shoulder at me. "Unfortunately, it looks like they're gone now. They must have slipped out when they saw us on the street."

"Fuck," I mutter as I lower my gun, scrubbing my free hand over my face. "Can you tell where they went?"

Jax throws a glance back in my direction, his snake-like eyes on full display. "I can sense thermal heat, but I'm not a fucking psychic," he says with a hiss. I roll my eyes as he turns away and continues moving through the house. "Use your fucking blood-hound to track their ass and let him suck them dry."

There's tension in the air, floating around us like dust particles as we stand at the bottom of the large staircase. Jax's fingers curl around the railing, but he freezes, his foot hovering over the first step. He stares up at the landing, undoubtedly holding his breath as his scales flicker across his skin. I reach up and rest my hand on his shoulder, and he stiffens under my touch.

"Hey, man, are you okay?" I ask, and at the sound of my voice, his muscles relax, letting out a ragged breath. But he doesn't respond. Instead, he begins his ascent up the stairs, taking each step with quiet precision.

I cover us from behind, the stairs creaking quietly under our weight as we make our way to the landing. The tension in the air grows heavy as we stare down the dark hallway. The only light comes from the moonlight shining through the window at the end of the hall, with the curtains fluttering from the cracked glass.

Jax moves through the hallway in complete stealth mode, checking behind every closed door while I watch the stairwell, occasionally looking at him over my shoulder. He takes a deep breath as he opens the second to last door, and I hear him gasp. "Atlas." He breathes my name as if the air has been squeezed from his lungs. "Come here. *Now*."

I keep my weapon up, my boots thudding softly on the thick runner rug that stretches the hallway, reaching him in just a few strides. He steps aside, the moonlight casting an eerie glow in the room as I enter, taking in every inch of the space. There's an old bed in the center of one wall, and it looks as if it's been slept in recently, the blankets rumpled and halfway on the floor. Next to it is a closet, the door cracked open enough that someone could be watching, but as I close in on the door, I pause, my eyes catching on something on the floor that is more than just clutter.

My jaw tenses as I take in the candles that are arranged in the middle of the room, their wicks still releasing a stream of smoke, as if they'd just been blown out. A thin circle of salt surrounds them, and a large, inverted pentagram is drawn in the center in black charcoal. I step further into the room and notice that the salt circle has been broken, my eyes following back to the cracked closet door.

"Atlas—" Jax whispers from where he stands behind me, but I cut him off by holding up my hand as I take a tentative step toward the closet. My fingers curl around the crystal knob while my other hand grips my gun, my finger resting on the trigger. My pulse quickens, and I steady myself; the silence in the room turning even heavier. I yank it open and simultaneously raise my gun, ready to take out whoever, or whatever, might be on the other side.

But instead of being met with a person, there's nothing but a few metal hangers and a broom in the corner. I let out a long exhale and take a step back, lowering my weapon to my side. "Someone was here, alright," I say, looking over my shoulder at Jax. "And not only were they watching us, but they were no doubt trying to summon something to kill us."

Jax eyes the summoning circle and shakes his head. "Those candles are still warm," he says, looking over his shoulder at the hallway. "But there's no one in the house now but us."

I shut the closet and turn to the bed, pulling up the sheets, searching for any clues. "They were staying here, and while I'd like to think they'll come back, I highly doubt it." I walk to the window that overlooks the street below. "And I have an eerie feeling that they're watching us—waiting for us to leave."

Jax walks up behind me, looking over my shoulder but staying silent as I turn to face him. "Did you say you checked Elara's apartment?" I ask, sliding my hand into my pocket, pulling out her bracelet, and holding it in my palm.

Jax eyes me warily. "I checked it right before I came to find you the other night. Why?"

"Did you actually go in and look around?"

He narrows his eyes, his pupils becoming slits. "Of course I fucking did. How else would I have known she really wasn't there?" His fingers curl into fists at his sides, squaring his shoulders, spreading his feet apart into a fighting stance.

Fucking Basilisks and their tempers.

I roll my eyes at him, the tension slithering off him. "Calm the fuck down, Jax," I say as I crouch down, assessing the symbol on the floor. "I think we should go back to her apartment and really look to see if anything's missing. Maybe that will help us figure out if she went willingly or if she was possibly kidnapped."

His boots enter my peripheral vision as he approaches. "What if someone sees us?" he asks, his body shifting slightly as anxiety pulses through the room like a beating heart. "What if they think we're the reason Elara is missing?"

I rise to my full height, meeting his gaze, his jaw tensing. "No one knows she's missing," I say as a matter of fact. "We go in there as if she's expecting us and take our time looking—no one will notice or suspect a thing. As long as you don't keep emitting your scent and give us away, we'll be fine."

His eyes shift back, pupils returning to regular size, as he runs his hands over his head, gripping his nape. "You're right," he huffs, "I'm sorry. Let's just go now before anything else happens out here." He looks down at the markings on the floor. "This place is freaking me the fuck out."

I chuckle as I slide Elara's bracelet back into my pocket, turning to leave when something catches my eye from where it sticks out from beneath the open bedroom door. Gripping the edge, I close it slightly and grab the spiral-bound notebook that lies face up on the floor.

The blue cover is worn, the corners of the pages curling up, and the wire of the spiral-bound edge is smashed. My eyes widen as I flip through the pages, seeing symbol after symbol roughly drawn on each page until they start to become more uniform. These symbols are just like the ones in the grimoires that I've seen Emilian flipping through, his brow creased as he works to figure out what they mean.

What the fuck?

My pulse pounds, and my hands start to tremble as I keep

flipping until I reach the last page. My eyes widen as I take in large block letters above a drawing of the same symbol that's carved onto my chest; it reads A-T-L-A-S.

Atlas.

JAX and I race through the city, sticking to the shadows as we hurry to Elara's apartment. Rounding the corner, we encounter a group of Knights gathered outside, laughing and carrying on. I glance at Jax, who takes a deep breath and rolls back his shoulders, his eyes shifting into those of his Basilisk form, almost daring one of them to give him a second glance.

Elara's apartment is considered public housing for the Knights. Unlike Jax and me, who have our own houses thanks to our families, many Knights move out of their family homes and into apartments scattered around the city. The recruits are required to share their communal space with members of their Legion in two and three-bedroom apartments on the lower floors. However, the higher levels of the building contain private, one-bedroom apartments for tenured Knights, such as Elara, where they can reside for as long as they remain actively serving.

As we approach, the group quiets down, making it clear that they're recruits who don't dare to step out of line when tenured Knights are present. They all stiffen as we pass, and I notice the whispers about Jax's eyes, awe in their voices. But as we climb the steps of the stoop, one of them calls out, "Hey!"

We both turn to see a kid, who seems to be freshly twenty-one, step out of the group. He has shoulder-length dark hair, half pulled up into a bun on top of his head, with his slightly pointed ears peeking out from the strands, revealing his Fae heritage. They're adorned with piercings that match those on his eyebrow and nose, with an array of tattoos that swirl up his arms, disappearing under the short sleeves of his shirt. "Aren't you the guy with the vampire for a pet?"

Jax tenses beside me, but I remain relaxed and run my hand through my hair. If this asshole thinks he's the first one to try to confront me about Emilian and throw me off guard, he's dead wrong. I slide my hand into my pocket and lean against the arch of the stoop, maintaining an air of casualness. "Who the fuck's asking?"

The half Fae gives me a shit-eating grin as he looks over to his comrades, who all wear terrified expressions. "Corrin," he says coolly, "I'm surprised you haven't heard of me, seeing as I'm a direct descendant of Grand Master Ransley." He raises his chin and crosses his arms over his chest, a glimmer of pride in his sharp eyes.

I give Jax a sidelong look as he crosses his arms, his stance relaxing as a sly smile creeps onto his lips. "Oh, I've heard of you," he says, showing off his scales. "My mother has told me stories of the long-forgotten bastard of the Grand Master, a stain on his once pristine reputation."

Corrin's jaw tenses, and his eyes narrow on us as Jax's words drift down the streets, encircling him and his friends. "Until you rise in the ranks, where maybe someday the Grand Master will notice you, I suggest you remember your fucking place," Jax hisses before turning and gliding into the building, the door swinging wide for me to catch it with my elbow.

I watch Corrin slink back toward his friends, mumbling something about us being self-righteous assholes as his hands curl into fists and his eyes flash with anger. But even with that expression, he knows better than to make a fool of himself. All it would take is one person telling the Grand Master that he's reminding the whole city he has a bastard running around to get him punished or exiled. Even though I don't know anything about my own family, the Fae are very particular about their lineage, and for Corrin to slip through is a dark mark on Ransley.

While most beings can mate outside of their own kind, it's nearly unheard of for the Fae. Corrin, however, is unlikely to find a Fae lover, since they're few and far between, and will likely be forced to choose a human from among his ranks—one that the council must approve so Corrin doesn't produce an offspring with too much power. These rules set by the council aim to prevent major power plays or usurpers from becoming powerful enough to take over the Knights by force—something that has only been attempted once, and have worked to make sure it never happens again.

I give him one last look and turn on my heel, following Jax as we make our way inside and up the endless flights of stairs to Elara's floor, holding onto the hope that she'll be there and that this will all have been a misunderstanding. But my heart sinks as we reach the top landing, passing the other doors, and round the corner to her private hall, only to see that her apartment door is ajar.

"Shit," Jax breathes behind me as I push open the door, revealing that not only is Elara not here, but the whole place has been ransacked.

15

6 MONTHS EARLIER

EMILIAN

ATLAS HAS BEEN PACING FOR WHAT SEEMS LIKE AGES, THE grandfather clock in the hall chiming for the tenth hour of the evening. I find my mind wandering from where I lounge in the study, counting the paces he makes from one end of the house to the other. I'm completely distracted by the sharp scent of his anxiety as it swirls through the air, pricking the inside of my nostrils. I keep my eyes down on the book that lies in my palm as I wait for him to decide that I've seen enough of the moon-light and need to return to my lair—away from him.

Until then, I plan to enjoy the ambiance the fire creates and the sight of Atlas lost in thought. As he walks by for the umpteenth time, I notice his furrowed brows and his murmurs growing louder. His ramblings would sound incoherent to others, but I catch every word as if it were whispered like sweet nothings directly into my ear.

"Emilian," he says from where he stands, his hand planted onto the doorframe. "If you were a Kelpie—"

I cock my head to the side. "But *I* am a vampire," I cut in, giving him a Cheshire smile. "You might consider me a pest, but I am far above those bottom feeders."

He groans and rolls his eyes. "I'm *well* aware," he says, crossing his arms and entering the room. "But just imagine that you *are* a Kelpie."

I shift on the chaise and sit up, gently closing my book before dropping it onto the pile at my feet. I do love the annoyed look on his face—the one where he's trying to work out a problem, not the one that's mixed with rage, like when he returns home from an extended mission or when he's struggling against his ever growing desires.

I lean back, extending my arm over the back of the seat, as if I'm a cat stretching after a long nap, kneading my claws into the fabric. "And what will I do as I pretend to be a Kelpie? Am I to imagine a swim in the river, the cool water rushing over my skin, or the squish of the dirt beneath my hooves as I enter the city proper?" I cross my ankle over my knee, tapping my muzzle with the pointer finger of my other hand. "Or am I in my human form, luring unsuspecting victims to their watery graves?"

The look of annoyance is permanently fixed on Atlas's face, and even if I tried, there's no removing the sly smile that's plastered onto mine, my fangs elongating from behind their cage, taunting him.

"Will you let me finish, or do I need to purchase a ticket for this production you're putting on?" he growls.

A laugh bubbles past my lips, almost getting caught inside my muzzle before ringing out into the room. "*That* was a good one," I say, a chuckle mixing with my words. "I need to remember it for when *you're* the one being insufferably dramatic." I give him a wink, eliciting another groan as he crosses to the desk, dropping into the chair.

And I'm the dramatic one.

"Seriously, Emilian, if you were a Kelpie, do you think you'd be brave enough to come into the city, or would you stay on the edge of it, where you're close enough to the banks of the Stygian River?"

I cock my head to the side. "Why do you ask?"

"We've had reports of a male who is walking through the city around sunset, soaking wet, and attempting to lure civilians into one of the alleys." He watches me as if he's politely waiting for an answer, but I can tell he's not done; the words are pressing against the inside of his mouth, begging to be let out, puffing his cheeks like a chipmunk.

I raise an eyebrow, and he huffs out a breath, running his hand through his already-tousled hair, stray pieces sticking up in every direction. "I just can't figure out how they're doing it. Where they're being spotted is too far from the river, and even if they made the trek at night, there's no way they could make it this far and stay wet." He turns to the framed map of Cindervail hanging above the mantle while he runs his other hand through his hair, gripping it at the roots. "They would die after being out of the water for that long, even in their human form."

I press my nails into the back of the chaise as I imagine his hand as mine, my fingers gripping his hair tightly and pulling his head back, exposing his throat to my bared fangs.

Hold yourself the fuck together, Emilian.

I blink and force myself to relax, replacing the image with that of a Kelpie, standing on the edge of the river, its dark hair matted to its face. Its cold eyes stare back while its lips pull into a sharp, terrifying smile that would make even mine look tame. I turn my attention to the map on the wall and push myself to my feet for a closer look.

I clasp my hands behind my back and follow the lines from the river into the city, admiring the infrastructure built to sustain us inside the wards. I continue tracing the city's layout, noting significant landmarks of my life as I focus on the location of this very townhouse. I think about my old life before I was forced to give it up for this one—the person I could have been before it was all ripped away by one drunken evening that led me down a dark alley and altered my life forever.

If only I had chosen a different street to walk home on, if only I'd listened to the bartender who told me to wait for an escort, then maybe I'd still be mortal, and maybe, just maybe, if fate had it, I would still have found Atlas. He would have seen me for who I am, not the monster that I've become, and our paths would be one he would yearn to walk alongside me on, basking in the sun to ripen and not rot as forbidden fruit.

Something clicks in my mind, pushing away the thoughts that threaten to send me into a spiral, as I look at the different colored lines on the map—the various paths that lead in and out of the city. "What if," I start, cocking my head to the side. "What if they're not making the trek *above* ground?" I look at Atlas over my shoulder. "What if they're coming in from *below*?"

He sits up, the leather chair squeaking, his eyes widening with realization as he jumps to his feet, joining me in front of the map. He points at the red lines that run into the city from the river, branching off in every direction like roots. "The water lines," he whispers. His head turns quickly in my direction, his usually stern face breaking into a wide, warm smile. "You're a fucking genius, Emilian." He turns toward me, wrapping his arms around me and holding me close in an embrace.

I stiffen, and as quickly as he pulls me in, he pushes me away. The bright smile disappears from his face, but instead of disdain in his gaze, it becomes heated. His jaw tightens as his arms drop to his sides, and we stare at one another, the tension building.

I can feel his pulse quicken, and a hint of desire wafts between us; the heated look in his eyes turns molten, burning bright like Hellfire. He closes the small distance between us, his hand coming up and hooking the O-ring on my collar. He holds my gaze as his fingers trail down from my chest to the laces of my pants, continuing past and cupping my hardening length.

I let out a quiet groan as he gently squeezes my cock, sending a jolt to my core that tingles up my spine. "Atlas," I say with a growl, my head becoming light as my desire takes hold, a hunger growling deep in my abdomen. "Wh—"

His brows climb up his forehead as he waits for me to finish, continuing to squeeze me through my pants, the words getting lost on my tongue. We're walking on a fraying tightrope, threatening to send us both plummeting to the ground, with the chance that neither of us will make it out of this alive.

He leans in, his nose pressing against my collar. "Cat got your tongue, Emilan?" he asks into the bars of my enclosure, his voice low, but where there's usually a bite, it's as smooth as honey dripping from his lips. "Were you about to say something?" he asks as he rubs his hand over my cock, the friction making me pant like a bitch in heat as he chuckles, the sound as dark as the moonless night. "That's what I fucking thought."

Unhooking his finger from the ring, he reaches around and undoes my muzzle, freeing me from its confinement as it falls to the floor with a clang, bouncing away and getting lost under the chaise. His mouth presses to mine, consuming me in a kiss and stealing my breath. His deft fingers undo the laces of my pants, letting them fall to the ground, exposing my throbbing cock, and roughly stroking me from tip to hilt.

I reach for his waistband, but he pushes my hand away, pulling back from the kiss and looking at me with wild eyes. His hand never stops as he continues to stroke my cock. "I'm going to make you come," he says roughly. "And then, I'm going to fuck you, so you remember *exactly* who you fucking belong to. Now, hands behind your back like a good pet."

His words nearly bring me to my knees, an audible groan slipping through my teeth, as I hold my hands behind me, my head falling back as pleasure washes over me in waves. He grips my collar, tugging my face back to his as he pulls me into another kiss, casting me under his spell. My mind races, trying to stay clear as the desire threatens to drown me.

What has gotten into him?

He hasn't been drinking tonight, so this kind of behavior is unusual for him in a sober state. Has he taken some of the edibles he hides in the cupboard? No, those are meant to help him relax, not turn him into a feral beast ready to sleep with someone he considers a nuisance.

A monster.

He drops his other hand to my chest, roughly pinching my nipple before flicking my piercing, eliciting another groan that he swallows whole as he glides his tongue past my lips—my fangs. The taste of his blood coats my tongue, and my eyes fly open, waiting for him to shove me away, but he only deepens the kiss.

And who am I to stop him?

My balls tighten, and the heat from my core climbs up my spine like a wildfire. His kiss pulls the air from my lungs as I thrust, coming hard into his hand, a growl rumbling between us. "Such a good little pet," he croons as he brings his glistening hand up to his lips, gliding his tongue through my cum, watching as it drips between his fingers. "And you say *I'm* delicious," he croons.

I'm panting and my knees have gone weak as everything I've wanted unfolds in front of me. I look at his hand that is now licked clean, my eyes flicking back to his, waiting for his next move. But the world nearly stops turning as his lips pull up into a cruel smile, his teeth sharpening as his irises go red, the whites of his eyes clouding with onyx smoke. I try to pull away, but his grip on my collar chokes me, holding me in place.

"You're not going anywhere, you piece of filth," he growls, his newly formed fangs glinting. His muscles ripple beneath his skin, growing larger with every blink, where he now towers over me. "Except back to Hell where you fucking belong."

His mouth widens, his jaw coming unhinged as he yanks the collar and lowers his fangs to the prominence of my neck, ready to tear me apart. He's no less a monster than I am. His thirst for blood—for *power*—is insatiable.

I attempt to scream, only for my eyes to open from where I lay in my bed, my legs tangled tightly in my sheets.

I sit up, gasping for breath, as my hand glides over my neck, looking for any traces of a bite, but I only feel the raised skin of the small scars that mar my throat. Warmth drips from between my legs, my cock throbbing and tender from the wet dream that maliciously dropped me into a nightmare. I look around the room, taking in every shadowy corner, everything still in its place, including the door to my enclosure—closed and locked tight, keeping the monsters in this house locked in…and out.

16

ATLAS

"What the fuck?" Jax whispers from where he stands behind me in the doorway, his hand planted firmly on my shoulder, ready to pull me back.

I flip on the lights, my gaze moving through the wrecked apartment. "Was it like this when you were here?" I ask. My chest tightens, and it feels as though a stone has dropped into the pit of my stomach.

I look at him over my shoulder, his mouth ajar, his eyes wide with shock. "No. *Fuck no.* Elara is a little messy, but this…" His eyes flicker around the room as we step into the apartment. "I would have fucking told you about *this.*"

It's as if a twister tore through her apartment. The furniture is turned upside down, all the cabinet doors are nearly ripped from their hinges, and every closet stands wide open, its contents dragged and scattered across the floor. Even the large area rug is flipped over, revealing what appears to be claw marks across the hardwood floor. I crouch down and run my fingers over the scratches; while they're deep, splintering the wood and almost breaking through, they're definitely not from a demon. It almost looks like…

The sound of heavy footsteps fills the hallway, panic flooding my veins. No, not footsteps...*hooves*.

My head snaps and I look at Jax, who stands frozen in the kitchen, staring at the still-open door behind me. I quickly flip the rug back over, concealing the claw marks, and race to Elara's bedroom door, closing it just as Chancellor Brander's large body fills the doorway. We both stand at attention as he steps through the threshold, barely making it through, and place our fists over our hearts while bowing our heads.

"Be at your leisure," he commands, his deep voice rumbling through the room. He's so large that his horns threaten to scrape the ceiling, with his thick, gold septum piercing shining. His muscles ripple as he takes careful steps, looking down at me from his height of over eight feet. "Sir Atlas," Brander starts, "would you care to explain what happened here?" His gaze shifts from mine to Jax, who has yet to leave the kitchen, his eyes moving back to me. "And where might Dame Elara be?"

Anxiety crawls across my skin as the feeling of fear heats up at the base of my neck. "Chancellor Brander, Sir," I say, giving a curt nod of my head out of respect, trying to bide my time as a flurry of explanations rushes through my mind, all of which he'd be able to see right through. I swallow thickly as I clasp my hands behind my back. "I—"

"We had a party here last night," Jax cuts in, crossing the room to my side. "And as you can see, it got a little rowdy." He nods toward the bedroom door. "Dame Elara has quite the hangover, and we came back to help clean up while she rests." Jax gestures around the apartment. "And as you can see, she needs all the help she can get."

What the fuck is Jax doing? As if Brander will ever believe that shit.

I turn my gaze in his direction just as he glances at me sideways, his serpent eyes narrowing to slits as if silently commanding me to be quiet. I've never seen him lie to a Chancellor, let alone hear one leave his lips so smoothly. Maybe he's more like me than I thought.

Brander looks down at both of us, his gaze cutting to Elara's closed bedroom door, and huffs out a breath so harshly through his nose that his piercing flutters. He gazes back at us with uncertainty in his eyes, and my lungs constrict as fear builds in my body. I grip my fingers so tightly behind my back that my knuckles quietly crack. seeming to make Jax wince.

Brander's body relaxes slightly, and his uncertainty morphs into annoyance. "While the two of you have ownership of your homes," he starts, "might I remind you that this is housing provided by the Vail and is to be treated *respectfully*." He steps closer to us, his large head and horns blocking the light that hangs above him, shadowing his face and making him look as terrifying as any demon I've ever encountered. "Now, clean this mess up and never let this kind of tomfoolery happen again. Do I make myself clear?"

Jax and I place our fists over our hearts and bow our heads, saying in unison, "Yes, Chancellor, Sir."

He huffs another breath as he steps back, delicately stepping over a pile of clothes, and turning toward the door to leave. My body begins to relax, and just as he gets to the doorway, he stops, turning back toward us. "Oh, and Sir Atlas, since you're present now, I don't have to hunt you down later," he says lowly. "Grand Master Ransley would like a word with you and your *pet* tomorrow evening. Please report to his chambers in the cathedral at 2200 sharp."

My heart stops in my chest, but I keep my face neutral, even as my neck begins to flush. "Of course, Chancellor," I reply, clasping my hands behind my back again, digging my nails into my palm. "Does he need reports on anything in particular?"

What could he fucking want? Meeting with him isn't an uncommon occurrence, as he likes to know what monsters are lurking in the streets. With my rising rank, he tends to speak with me more often than most, but it's out of character for him to request Emilian's presence as well.

Brander narrows his eyes slightly, as if trying to sense any lies or deceit, as he's more wary of humans than many other beings. The tension grows between us as he stares me down, but I keep my hands clasped and my shoulders relaxed. Jax shifts on his feet next to me, his scales pressing against his skin, his own tell that he's just as anxious as I am.

Brander's eyes shift in his direction, breaking his gaze from me, the tension slowly dissipating as he takes in the Basilisk at my side, his lip curling up in a slight snarl. "Not that I'm aware of, however, he didn't disclose anything to me. Is there anything *I* need to know to report back to him?"

His gaze cuts to Jax, making it obvious that he isn't privy to sharing any Legion business with anyone outside our ranks, so I shake my head. "Of course not, Chancellor, Sir. I just didn't want to arrive ill-prepared, that's all."

He narrows his gaze at me again, a flame as bright as the torch on our signet burning in his eyes, but in a blink, it's gone. He turns back toward the door, huffing out another breath. With his hand on the door, he says, "Very well, I bid you both good nights, and I expect this apartment spotless the next time I choose to visit. Is that clear?"

"Yes, Sir," we say in unison again as he steps back through the threshold and snaps the door shut behind him, a wave of relief washing over us.

Jax and I look at one another. "Holy shit," he breathes. "That was *really* fucking close."

I turn to him fully, my brows knitted together. "I didn't know you were such a good fucking liar," I say, quirking a brow. "I'll say, I'm impressed."

He stands quietly, looking around before bending over to pick up a photo of a large group of Knights from the night we were initiated. Elara's arms are wrapped around mine and Jax's necks, pulling all three of our heads together, bright smiles plastered on our faces from where we stand right in the middle. That night was nothing more than a blur of alcohol and questionable decisions before we went full steam ahead into Knighthood. He glances between me and the photo, his eyes softening before letting his arm fall to his side, the frame still pinched between his fingers.

I turn away, leaving him to his thoughts, my own anxiety prickling my skin like a thousand needles. I look around, and immediately my anxiety is replaced with a flicker of anger as my mind fills with so many questions that we still don't have answers for.

Who the fuck did this? Where is she? Why hasn't she tried to contact us?

My boots stomp on the floor as I cross to Elara's bedroom door, wrenching it open. "We can't waste any more time, Jax, especially now that Brander was here," I say over my shoulder. "Someone was clearly looking for something, and I don't feel like they found it. Now, we need to see if anything is missing or looks out of the ordinary."

I hear Jax grumble from where he stands back in the living room as I yank open her dresser drawer and start sifting through her clothes, searching for any clues. "Wherever she went, something isn't too far behind, and we have to find her before it's too late," I say loudly enough for him to hear.

I sense Jax at the doorway behind me, but I don't turn as I keep rifling through her dresser, looking for hidden compartments or anything she might be hiding. Jax clears his throat, and I finally turn to see him standing with his arms crossed tightly over his chest, his brows furrowed.

"*What?*" I ask, anger seeping into my tone.

He takes a few steps into Elara's room, looking at her unmade bed and tracking the mess of things thrown across the floor. "What if..." He takes a breath, scrubbing his hand over his face. "What if Elara isn't in trouble?"

I freeze, my heart thundering in my ears, my cheeks heating

with rage as it begins to pulse through my veins. "What the fuck, Jax?" I bite out, my voice turning rough. "Of course she's in fucking trouble. Look at this place."

He takes a few more steps toward me, his body tensing. "Think about it, Atlas," he says, squaring his shoulders. "She disappeared without a trace, and suddenly, all these demons and monsters started appearing, as if someone was trying to lead us away from the city. We just found a fucking summoning circle in the same neighborhood where you captured your vampire, and the person who did it slipped away as if they knew we would go around to the back door. Not to mention the sinkhole that conveniently tore open the alley. Don't you think it's a little suspicious?"

I stare at him, my jaw tensing as I try to find the words to explain all this away, but they keep shriveling up my tongue. I know Elara isn't capable of anything like this. She's a fucking Knight of the Vail and my oldest friend. Are things complicated with us right now? Yeah, but that doesn't make her a traitor or my enemy.

"Jax, you're fucking—"

He steps forward, pushing his finger into my chest, his pupils sharpening into slits. "*Your* name was in that notebook, Atlas, next to the same symbol that's carved into your fucking chest. Do you really believe that it's a coincidence?"

I look down at where his finger presses into me, white hot rage filling my veins. "Just because my name was in there doesn't mean it was Elara's doing. For all we know, they could have been using me as bait to lure her out there. Everyone knows my name in this city because I'm the freak with the fucking vampire."

I can feel my face redden as I push his finger away from my chest, and something unfamiliar blooms in my chest, the words scratching against my throat. "Maybe they promised her they could get rid of him and free me from my bargain. I know everyone loathes his existence, especially Elara, and sees him as an enemy, but even if I wanted to, I can't get rid of him. He's not just a fucking pet—he's an asset to the Vail."

Jax cocks his head to the side, his expression softening as his pupils widen. "No one's asking you to get rid of him, Atlas." This time, when he reaches out and grips my shoulder, he gives it a gentle squeeze. "I don't know why Elara hates him so much —that's her business. And even though he's a blood-sucking monster, and I still don't know how you managed to capture him, he's never hurt you, and you seem to trust him. So, by extension, I seemingly trust him, too. If I'm being honest, I think he's actually kept you safe this entire time, because you always seem to be doing extra stupid shit when he's around." A ghost of a smile pulls up at his lips, his serpent eyes flashing, causing a warmth to swirl in my chest.

He gives me a soft grin. "And he's been more than willing to help us search for Elara, who has never been shy about her detestation for him. And I'm not going to lie, he puts me on edge, but I think it's a lot of my Basilisk instincts. Two predators of different species together don't usually bode well for anyone involved, but he's never hesitated to step in, especially to protect *you*. He might be a monster, but he seems like a pretty loyal one to me."

I stare at him, dumbfounded, because he's right...about everything.

Emilian has always been my ally, yet I've treated him as if he's nothing more than a pest that needs to be eradicated. He's always gleefully given whatever I've needed, but I've taken far more than my fair share from him. He's never deserved the way I've treated him over the last decade, and I can't deny the ache in my chest every time I pull away, as if my body is begging me to stay with him. As if it's trying to tell me that I need him for more than just to find release from my own demons, and that he needs me more than just to feed on my blood.

I avert my gaze and squeeze my eyes shut, trying to clear my mind, but all I can see are red eyes looking back at me, staring deep into my soul. A sharp mouth forms, lips curling back to expose pearly white fangs, while a warm breath brushes against the column of my throat, and a musky scent fills my nostrils. Phantom fingers fill the spaces between mine, ready to lead me down the narrow path between life and death.

My heart thunders in my chest as I open my eyes and face Jax, his eyes filled with concern. I run my hand through my hair, pulling at the roots, letting the sharp pain ground me. "Let's keep looking for any more clues and get the fuck out of here, okay? Elara can clean this shit up herself."

I move past Jax and try to pull open the drawer of her nightstand, but it doesn't budge. "What the fuck?" I mutter as I yank on it again until it finally slides out. I dig through it, my hand moving around an array of vibrators, random cough drops, and lip balms, clearing the way to reveal a black leather notebook that has been purposefully hidden away under a stack of tissues.

My fingers curl around it, sliding it out and holding it up. It's old, the leather dry and cracked, and the pages inside yellowed with time. The spine cracks loudly as I open it, revealing page after page of someone's handwriting. The script is sharp, as if they couldn't get the words on the pages fast enough.

A journal, maybe?

No...*a grimoire.*

17

ATLAS

"What's that?" Jax asks from over my shoulder as I try to read the fading ink, slowly flipping through the pages. The symbols elegantly drawn inside seem far too familiar.

"A journal," I say simply, the white lie flowing from my lips so easily.

"Elara's?" he asks, staring down at where it lies open in my hand.

I close it slowly, careful not to cause any more damage to the already delicate pages, and slide it into my jacket pocket. "I don't know whose it is, and it's old, like, really old, but definitely not hers."

He looks down at her nightstand drawer. "Whatever tore apart her apartment obviously missed the good stuff." He scoffs a laugh before turning on his heel and leaving the room. I listen as he starts rummaging through the kitchen, his boots crunching over broken glass, the sound of drawers sliding open and closed filling the space between us.

I clutch my fingers around the grimoire, pulling it back out of my pocket and turning it over in my hands, noticing a single word written in smooth script on the front page: *Delvaux*. My heart hammers in my chest, causing my ribs to ache as I trace my finger over the word. There's a pressure pulsing between my eyes, as if a memory is trying to push its way out.

Why do you have this, Elara?

I snap it shut again and shove it back in my pocket. I drop to my knees and blindly rummage under the bed, but there's nothing more than a box of old photographs from our childhood, with more recent photos scattered on top, along with a litter of dust bunnies. I rise back to my feet and curl my hand around the bracelet, rubbing my thumb over the rubies before dropping them back into the nightstand drawer and slamming it closed.

An even trade.

The grimoire in my pocket sits heavy, making my skin heat with whatever magic is written among its pages. A knot forms in my chest as if it's caught in a vise, attempting to crush me. Maybe Emilian knows something about it, and we can figure it out together. But right now, we need to track down what's hunting Elara and why it's so hellbent on finding her.

I look around her room, the pressure in my forehead spreading, pulsing through my skull and down my neck. I squeeze my eyes shut as memories that don't seem to be my own flash in my mind. The pieces start to click together, the blurred edges finally clearing, turning sharp as my bottled-up anger begins to flow into my veins.

"Jax," I call out as I leave the bedroom, stomping my boots over the mess. He jumps up from where he was crouched behind the kitchen peninsula and drops a stack of plastic cups, clattering across the floor. "Let's go," I say, heading toward the front door.

Jax rounds the counter, brushing his hands off on his pants. "What's the rush?" He looks around, his skin shimmering with scales, ready to strike.

I stop at the door, gripping the handle tightly, the veins on the back of my hand pulsing. "We're going to get Emilian." I glance over my shoulder, my words growing sharper, almost as if they're growing teeth. "And I think I know where Elara might be."

EMILIAN REMAINS in the shadows as we move through the city proper. Civilians are closing their homes for the evening, adhering to the curfew imposed by the Grand Master amid the rise in attacks. A few wave politely at us, unaware of the vampire lurking in the dark corners of the street, while others spot him right away and hurry inside, the sound of their dead-bolts echoing like gunshots.

"Tough crowd tonight," Jax says, chuckling darkly as the last of the shutters and doors slam shut, the street falling dead quiet.

The buildings around us begin to change as we enter the abandoned part of the city, shifting from the modern skyscrapers and well-maintained structures to those with crumbling façades and cracked cobblestone streets littered with debris. We approach the house I often see in my dreams, where Emilian is already standing at the bottom of the stoop, staring up at the door. He inhales deeply through his nose, not bothering to look over at us as he says, "Someone's in there."

I scan the building, looking for subtle movements that might imply an ambush, but everything is still—*hushed*. The last of the daylight dips beyond the horizon, with only the glow of sparse streetlights reflecting off the windows. My gaze shifts to Emilian as he slowly ascends the steps, and I admire the sheer power he emits, his muscles pressing against his leathers. I removed his muzzle at home, where he barely looked me in the eyes, his anger still palpable, but he didn't object when I said I needed his help—proving once again that he's more of a hero than I would be.

I wanted to apologize, fall to my knees, and tell him that I've been a fucking asshole and he deserves better. But the words kept getting lost, fizzling out on the tip of my tongue, as if afraid to fill the uncomfortable silence that sits between us. Once the muzzle was removed, he sidestepped me to the door, not even acknowledging Jax as he left the house.

The ache in my chest grows, making it harder to ignore as the symbol etched into my skin heats. Instead of dwelling on it, I focus on scouting out the street, covering for Emilian at the front while Jax moves stealthily around back, both of us determined not to let the culprit escape this time.

I move in, gun raised as I walk backward up the steps, while Emilian twists the handle, the door quietly creaking open. He passes through the threshold, wincing slightly as if the abandoned house is trying to keep him from entering, but he moves through the foyer and stops at the bottom of the stairs.

A quiet hiss fills the hall as Jaxon moves through, already on the verge of shifting, his scales glimmering. Emilian locks eyes with me for the first time, truly looking at me. Unlike his usual mischievous expression, his gaze remains intense, his red irises flickering like the flames of Hell.

It only took him a decade to see what a real piece of shit I am, and no matter what the Grand Master wants from both of us tomorrow, I think it's time I let him go. Let him finally be free from me and the life that I've forced him to live. I'll ensure he has a safe place to go, maybe with the small coven outside of the city, so he can continue his immortal life, but this time in peace.

It will tear me apart to let him leave, and thinking about it already feels as if I'm cutting out part of my soul. But I did this to myself by not giving him the respect he wholly deserves and playing into the role everyone expected of me. He's never been my enemy. If anything, he's the only one who seems to truly understand me and has never passed judgment like so many others would have.

I keep his gaze as I hold a sledgehammer to the walls that I've worked so hard to maintain between us, smashing the heavy metal straight through them, and finally letting them crumble around me, showing him who I truly am underneath it all—baring myself to him.

His eyes narrow slightly, and his mouth opens as if he wants to say something, but the soft creak of the floorboards above us interrupts the heavy silence. All three of us look up as a small cloud of dust drifts down like ash, a smoke signal that we weren't just hearing things.

Emilian moves with a predatory quiet as he makes his way up the stairs, Jax on his heels. I wait for them to reach the top, noting exactly where they stepped on each step, hoping that I don't hit the one creaky board in the whole fucking house and give us away.

As we near the top, I hear a soft voice and catch a glimpse of flickering light from under the door at the end of the hall. Jax turns, tilting his head in that direction, and I give him a brief nod as I raise my gun. He moves past Emilian to grasp the door handle and looks over his shoulder just as he is yanked into the room with a loud yelp.

18

ATLAS

I GASP AND TRY TO RUSH TOWARD THE DOOR, BUT BEFORE I CAN move, Emilian grabs my jacket collar and yanks me back. I slam into the opposite wall as he storms into the room, the air forced from my lungs as I struggle to keep my knees from buckling. I take a ragged breath and lunge for the door again, as a roar shakes the house, nearly knocking me off balance.

I grip the doorframe as I come face to face with a demon like I've never seen before. Its tar-slicked body is slender, but beneath it, its skin glows like crackling embers. Its eyes are just holes in its face, lit by flames, and black, jagged horns curl around its head, with one piercing into the back of its skull.

A scream pierces the room as Elara cowers in the corner, covering her head. I look down just as the demon steps out of the broken summoning circle, its massive, clawed feet scraping across the charcoal of the pentagram, sealing the rift it has just emerged from. The demon's fiery eyes lock onto me, a grin spreading across its face to reveal rows of razor-sharp teeth, while its long tongue flicks out to lick its thin lips.

"Atlas," Emilian growls where he stands beside me, my name sounding almost like a desperate plea. "Leave. *Now.*"

I cut him a sidelong glance as the demon looks between us,

sniffing the air, its smile growing wider—*crueler*. "Ah," it starts, its voice echoing through the room. "A pair of *lovers*. That will make you that much sweeter when I devour you both whole." Its claws lengthen as it extends its arms, appearing to grow larger, while its horns scrape the ceiling. "But which one will I take first?"

"Atlas, *go*," Emilian growls again, his own claws growing sharper as his fangs elongate, the whites of his eyes turning a deep onyx, his red irises glowing with rage.

The demon laughs, its sound rattling the windows as a venomous hiss cuts through the air. The demon turns its head just as Jax attempts to strike, but is stopped when the demon grips him by the throat and throws him across the room as if he's nothing more than a small garden snake, knocking him unconscious. Elara screams again as the drywall crumbles around him, the glass in the window splintering as shards fall on top of him.

The demon turns back to us, its eyes shining brighter as if lighter fluid had been poured over its head. I stand my ground, pointing my gun right at its chest, armed with our issued silver bullets. It looks down at it, its body burning brighter as my hand heats, the smell of burning flesh filling my nose as the barrel of my gun melts in my hands. I choke out a scream and stumble back, dropping it at my feet where it continues to melt into a puddle of molten steel, the liquid bubbling and burning a hole through the floor.

"Not so powerful now, are you, little witch?" The demon's voice echoes in my head, and I can see Emilian's head whip around, his eyes widening as he looks between the demon and me. "And here I thought you would be somewhat of a challenge, given the history of your family." It stalks toward me, the flames in its eyes dancing. "It's too bad you're the last of them. I've heard they were quite delectable—a rare delicacy."

It reaches for my throat, its claws lengthening more, and even as I try to will my legs to move, for my body to do anything, I'm frozen in place. "And now, I will feast upon the flesh of the last living heir of the Delvaux coven. It's been said their blood is the sweetest of them all." It laughs, the sound chilling my bones. I squeeze my eyes shut, ready for the pain that it's about to inflict on me, but it doesn't come. Instead, a familiar roar fills my ears along with the sound of claws scraping across the hardwood floor.

"*Emilian,*" I scream as my eyes fly open, his claws and fangs tearing at the demon's chest and throat. Its roar shakes the house as its claws sink into Emilian's back, attempting to pull him off. They crash into the back wall, becoming a tangle of teeth and claws. The plaster crumbles before falling away, with gravity taking hold like a clawed hand and dragging them to the street below.

"*Emilian. No,*" I scream, my body finally freed from whatever hold the demon had on me. I stumble forward, gripping the jagged edges of the gaping hole, a plume of dust filling the air below. Emilian and the demon's roars fill the street, proving that they're both still alive. Fear grips me, and my eyes widen, tears filling the corners as the dust hits my face.

"Atlas," Elara says with a sob as she gets to her feet, his eyes wide.

I turn to her as rage ignites within me. I rush at her, gripping her shoulders and shaking her. "What did you fucking do, Elara? What is that thing?" Her mouth opens and closes like a fish out of water, her eyes widening more, her body trembling. "And how do we fucking stop it?"

Her bottom lip quivers as silver lines her eyes. "I...I don't know," she says as a sob racks through her. "Atlas, I'm sorry. You have to believe me."

Another roar pierces the air, followed by a deep, dark chuckle that filters up, swirling into the room with a gust of wind. My body aches with pain as if my ribs are cracking one by one and piercing my skin. I let go of Elara and double over, grunting in pain as I try to catch my breath.

What the fuck is happening?

Now awake and on his feet, Jax steps between us, resting his hand on my back before looping his arm around my center and holding me up. I turn my head and look up at him, seeing the blood as it trickles down his face from his temple.

"It's been you this whole fucking time," Jax hisses as he looks Elara up and down, his scales rippling across his skin as his eyes narrow on her. "You've been opening up portals and letting demons through. You've been trying to lure us out here to kill us. You're a fucking *traitor*."

She stifles a sob as she backs against the only remaining part of the wall. "I didn't mean for it to go this far. You have to believe me. *Please*."

Jax moves closer to her, his arm slipping away as he grips her shoulder and drags her to the blown-out wall, forcing her to look down. "Do you see what you've fucking done? And for what? Why did you fucking do this, Elara?"

She looks over her shoulder at me, her eyes narrowing. "Because that blood-sucking leech was ruining you, Atlas." Her voice is sharp, the words like a blade at my chest. "He was making you *weak*, and you were letting him fucking consume you. I've seen the fucking teeth marks. And I couldn't handle you pulling away from me for that *monster*." She lets loose another sob, her tear-stained face flushed. "He has been driving a wedge between us for years. And I just thought that if I lured you both out here, he would be caught off guard, and you'd be rid of him for good, like you've always wanted. Like *we* always wanted. And then you and I—"

I let out a growl, the sound clawing up my throat and charging past my lips as my anger grows, trying to take on a life of its own. "That's what this is all about?" I heave in a breath, my head spinning as I think back to the days leading up to her disappearance. "Because you were fucking *jealous*?"

She turns to face me, her expression morphing from innocent fear to a feral rage in a single blink. "We've known each other since we were babies, Atlas. Don't you see that we were *destined* to be together?"

"You've had a fucking boyfriend, Elara," I roar. "Did he even cheat on you, or was that some sob story—a fucking lie?"

Her eyes flash as her hands curl into fists at her side. "You weren't paying attention to me. You were always locking yourself away with that piece of fucking filth." She shoves a finger into my chest. "I saw what he was doing to you. He was using his allure to keep you right where he wanted you, and I thought that once I finally convinced you to fuck me—"

Jax's body shifts, his eyes wide as he battles to maintain his human form. "You *what*?" He glances between us as another roar echoes through the alley below. It won't be long now before someone is notified, and Knights will be swarming this place. Emilian's life hangs in the balance.

I open my mouth, but instead of words, a manic laugh pushes past my teeth and lips, a sharp pain piercing through my chest. "This is fucking rich," I bite out. "Putting us in real danger with a demon, all because you couldn't stand that I was spending more time with a vampire. You're more of a fucking monster than he has ever been."

"I was trying to save you, Atlas. *Free* you," she cries, but I see right through her crocodile tears.

"Your game is over, Elara. *We're* over." I point to the massive hole in the wall, my hand shaking with fury and fear. "Stop this *now*."

"I know what you are, Atlas," she says coolly, her demeanor shifting right before my eyes. "You could be great. *Powerful*. Live out the legacy that was laid for you. But instead, you're letting your pity bargain with that creature ruin everything. Ruin *you*."

I stare at her, my jaw tensing, my teeth nearly cracking. It all makes so much sense now. I let her roam free in my home, giving her years to figure out what I so ignorantly ignored. She stole the clues that Emilian tried to give me about my past to use as ammunition for her future. Everything about me, about my life, is nothing more than a fabrication, a lie—except for one thing.

The floor beneath us shakes. Emilian's roar fills my ears as another pang of pain hits my chest. "We have to help Emilian!" I roar, locking eyes with Jax.

I turn on my heel and race out of the room, flying down the stairs, and turning toward the exit at the back of the house, Jax hot on my heels. Elara betrayed me and our entire Legion—the whole city. Her jealousy and power trip made her nearly as monstrous as the demon she summoned.

She's as good as dead to me.

I yank open the back door and stop in my tracks, taking in the sight before me, and the pain radiating from my chest settles into my bones. Emilian lies face down as he struggles to push himself back to his feet. The slashes across his body aren't healing as they usually do, and blood is pooling around him. The demon moves swiftly, grabbing Emilian by the hair and wrenching his head back.

"Your little witch is here now, leech. He's just in time to watch you be dragged back to Hell, where you fucking belong." It chuckles darkly as it wraps its hand around Emilian's throat, flipping him onto his back and holding him in place. Emilian claws at the demon's hand and struggles against its hold, but it's no use. "There's only one true way to kill a vampire, and your little witch provided me with just the thing."

The demon raises a wooden stake into the air—the very one that I rammed into the other demon's skull. It's now singed and stained as black as a demon's blood, with the carved symbols shining bright in the moonlight.

I think back to the night I made it, years ago, while sitting in the study with Emilian. He casually flipped through a book and told me which symbols to carve, promising that it would end everything if I ever needed to use it. Panic wraps tightly around me as the demon lifts the stake above his head and drives it into Emilian's chest, lodging it right into his undead heart.

19

3 MONTHS EARLIER

EMILIAN

I RACE THROUGH THE DENSE FOREST THAT SURROUNDS THE CITY, dodging fallen trees and leaping over creeks, leaving the towering skyscrapers behind as I run freely through the wild land just inside the wards. The bright light of the full moon fills the open spaces of the canopy, illuminating the forest floor and making it even easier to spot my prey.

A low growl in the distance catches my attention, prompting me to veer off in its direction. The scent of blood being carried by the wind fills my nostrils, making my mouth water. I follow the aroma and the sound of the low growls as I move toward a clearing. I slow my steps and quietly approach the tree line as snarls and snapping teeth disrupt the otherwise quiet night. I watch as two rogue wolves circle one another, utterly oblivious to the true predator observing them, planning its own attack.

They're both dripping blood, their lips curled into vicious snarls. I've entered a waiting game to see which one will fall first, and I enjoy a good game—especially when the boredom of being locked in the basement edges me toward insanity. Tonight, the muzzle is off, and the leash is unclipped.

I thoroughly plan to have my cake and eat it, too.

Even muzzled, I can play my own games with Atlas. I do

enjoy pushing his boundaries and discovering more of what makes him tick, all while slowly chipping away at his tough exterior. My intrigue has only grown over the years as I've watched him mature and attempt to figure himself out.

Something he's been doing a terrible job of.

He believes he knows himself, but I understand him better. He functions like clockwork, day after day, only to break from routine when he reaches a weak spot and seeks relief—or release. He's growing angrier with himself and stretching out the days between visits even further, as if he can convince himself he doesn't need me in the same way I need him.

Our bargain is life-binding, but if his fellow Knights ever caught on to his proclivities for the monster that goes bump in the night, well, that could be the end for both of us. It's no secret I reside in his home, but vampires are illegal in this city, with only a few being allowed to dwell in their coven far away from everyone. I would rather be dragged to Hell than ever live with them.

My worst memory floods my mind, and I can still smell the rain-soaked concrete and feel the scrape of the bricks against my back. I can see the shadow of the man whose voice caressed my skin and filtered into my mind, luring me down the dark alley. I can't see his face that's hidden by the shadows, but I can still hear his deep, rough voice with its promise of pleasure, only to be left in a pool of my own blood, my old life sucked from me. He intended to leave me for dead, but something went very wrong for both of us, and he left me to fend for myself.

I know my sire is still in the city, and he must be a man of power to slip away from his crime unscathed. If he isn't, I imagine the Knights have already destroyed him—a quiet sacrifice in the name of their city. Either way, I stopped looking a long time ago, letting the answers I desperately craved die with my old life.

While he stole so much from me that night, I didn't really have much going for me, either. My parents were already dead, and the whole reason I was out was because I walked in on who I thought was the love of my life sleeping with another man, one who acted surprised himself to see me walk through the door, a key clutched in my hand. I told him to gather his belongings and leave as I turned and left, my world crashing down and burning around me.

He was gone when I came stumbling back as a completely different creature, the apartment cleared of his things. My need for blood was insatiable, my teeth aching from my newfound fangs, and I was sincerely hoping that they would still be there for an easy meal. He disappeared into the night, just like the monster who changed me, never to be seen again—that is, until a few years later when we reunited on his drunken walk home.

However, unlike me, he didn't get a second chance.

I had managed to stay in my old home, hidden away and retreating into the forest to feed when the need became too great, until that fateful night I ran into Atlas. From that moment on, my entire life changed. It was a relief not to have to keep living in the house that shattered me—changed me. And thankfully, it's on the other side of the city, so I don't have to be constantly reminded of the evening filled with nothing but bitter betrayals.

A growl slices through the air, pulling me from my thoughts, and I see the wolves are at it again, their jaws dripping with blood as they try to tear each other apart. They're equal in size, so it will come down to who gets the lucky bite to claim their victory. However, no one is winning tonight except for me, as I intend to drink my fill and distract myself from the one thing I truly crave.

I watch as the wolves battle it out until finally, one makes a misstep as the other sinks its teeth into its throat, ripping it out and killing it almost instantly. The smell of their blood mixes in the air, and while it smells delectable, it's nothing compared to Atlas's—sweet as the nectar of the gods. This will satisfy my hunger and leave me somewhat filled, while his seems to leave me wanting more, deepening our connection and fueling my insatiable desire.

The wolf shifts back into his human form, falling to his knees, his heavy breaths filling the air. I note the claw marks across its chest, slashing through a tattoo that is too mangled to make out. He's obviously a lone wolf, banished from his pack for whatever act of treason he committed. By the looks of it, he's been out here a while. I don't know much about the wolf shifters, but I know their rules are strict, rarely offering anyone a chance to come back.

What a pity that he won't get the chance to appeal their decision.

I take a step closer to the clearing, and his head snaps up, but not in my direction. He looks over his shoulder as the wind carries sharp voices from the distance, making this hunt riskier now that it's not just me and the lone wolf.

Well, fuck.

I've already spent so much time hunting for the perfect bite that I'll have to find another meal on my way back to the city, where Atlas is set to meet me an hour before sunrise.

I step back, the breeze tousling the leaves and carrying a scent that makes me stop in my tracks. It's familiar, but is mixed with someone else's, making it hard to decipher from this distance, especially as it blends with the blood of the wolves. Their sharp whispers grow louder as the wolf backs into the other side of the clearing, disappearing between the trees and fleeing into the night, leaving his kill out in the open for the taking.

I have a few moments before the unknown voices pose a threat, so I seize the opportunity and move into the clearing, the other wolf now far enough away not to detect my scent. I crouch and run my hand over the dead wolf's fur, its still-warm blood coating my hand, as its lifeless eyes stare into the starless sky. Suddenly, I'm not as hungry or desperate for a meal as I once thought I was.

I am not a vulture who needs to pick off the scraps of other exiles to survive.

I do not need to live up to the title of vermin that Atlas has so eloquently bestowed upon me, and I ignore the claws of hunger as they dig into me.

A twig snaps, causing the forest to fall silent as the wind dies down. I rise slowly, taking a deep breath as the mysterious scent becomes undeniable, close enough to recognize as one that has floated through the cracks in the floor, right into my dwelling. My steps backward into the woods are deliberate, as the murmurs from the other side of the clearing draw nearer.

I would recognize one of those murmurs like I know my own after the years they have spent in our house, but the other? It's deep and rough, yet not one I can place in my memory.

I should stay and see if my suspicions are correct, but I catch a glimpse of the moon as it peeks through the canopy, lowering itself and giving me its warning. If I want to find something to hold me over, then I need to get back to hunting, as it seems that time is not on my side tonight.

I hear a low, rough growl, followed by a quiet gasp, the sound quickly muted. I glance over my shoulder toward the clearing, but all that remains is the body of the lone wolf, its blood staining my hands—another reason to leave. I don't want to end up on trial for murder with one of the packs, as their courts run separately from the laws of the city, and the Grand Master allows their verdicts to stand. And even though it's an exiled member, if they discover me out here alone, they'll find any excuse to shove a stake through my heart and watch the afterlife leave my eyes for good.

The sound of another twig snaps, echoing like a warning I should heed. Without a second glance, I take off on near-silent feet, leaving whatever is unfolding behind me. It's not my business, nor do I care who anyone else is with, as long as they don't lay a finger on what's mine.

20

ATLAS

"*EMILIAN!*" HIS NAME TEARS AT MY THROAT AS I RACE TOWARD him, a hole in my own chest gaping open as I feel the life slipping away from him. The demon turns and gives me a wicked grin just as Jax strikes, sinking his venomous fangs into the demon's side. It roars, the sound shaking the ground beneath our feet as it slashes its claws at Jax, their blood mingling in the alleyway.

Shouts erupt from the far end of the street as three figures rush toward us. Their faces are a blur, but I hear growls, one of them howling as they charge the demon. I don't turn to watch; instead, I slide to Emilian's side, the rubble digging into my knees.

"Emilian," I choke out as I stare down at him, his eyes slowly opening. They're glazed over, his pupils narrowing, his red irises almost as full as the moon that hangs above us.

I grip his face, pushing back his hair. "*Emilian.* Emilian, please." I glide my hands down to his chest, everything around me blurring as I stare at the stake in his chest, blood seeping around it, the skin peeling back as if it's been singed by the very Hellfire that made him. Looking back at his face, my stomach drops as his eyes flutter closed.

"No. No. No. *No*." I grip his face, forcing him to look at me. "Stay with me, Emilian. *Please*."

He forces his eyes open, his gaze going distant. "Atlas," he breathes, his voice barely above a whisper. "I'm…I'm sorry."

I shake my head, shushing him as I brush my fingers past his lips, wiping away a small dribble of blood. "No, Emilian. *I'm sorry*. I'm sorry for everything. I've been a fucking asshole to you, and I-I never meant any of it." I suck in a ragged breath; the roars and growls of the fight behind us are muted as I focus on him. "Tell me what to do. *Please*."

The corners of his lips tip up, showing his fangs. "But you hate when I do that."

I shake my head at his attempt at a joke, my chest burning. "Emilian, *please*. Tell me what to do. I'll do anything. *Anything*." A sob breaks loose, and the tears that I had been holding back spill over and splash onto his face. "Just don't leave me," I choke out.

He raises his hand, resting it on my chest, right over the symbol. "Balance," he says roughly. "It's all about balance."

My cheeks flush as I push back his hair again, letting the silky strands wrap around my fingers. "I don't fucking care about balance, I care about *you*. I need *you*." I look up as the ground shakes and see that Jax, along with the backup—a Legion of wolf shifters—now has the demon on his knees, his roar deafening as they continue to tear him apart piece by piece.

I turn my attention back to Emilian, the veins around his eyes blackening. "You have to choose, Atlas," he whispers. "The balance of life and death…*you* have to decide."

I stare at him, the words sinking in as if they're fangs bared at my throat. The pain in his eyes is unlike anything I've ever felt as it reverberates through me, making my own body tremble. "I've been a fucking fool, Emilian. You've always deserved better than me. I'm the real monster, and I want to spend lifetimes making it up to you." I cup my hand around his nape, lifting him to me. He groans in pain as I pull him in, carefully resting his chin on my shoulder. "I choose you, Emilian. *All* of you." I swallow around the lump that forms in my throat as tears prick behind my eyes. "I was a fucking fool not to see that it's *always* been you."

His body trembles against mine. "Death is far too welcoming, Atlas," he breathes into my ear. "But it's not always kind as it drags you under."

I tilt his head, letting his lips brush against my neck. "Take my life for yours," I gently grip his hair, angling my head away, giving him better access to my throat. "I'll gladly pay the price so long as this world has you in it."

His fangs scrape against my skin as his body grows heavier in my arms, his skin heating up as if he's on fire. "There's no going back, Atlas," he says sternly. "And there could be dire consequences."

I grip his hair tighter, pressing his mouth against my neck, not letting him pull away. "Do it, Emilian," I growl. "Before it's too late. Fucking do it *now*."

The ground beneath us shakes as a roar fills the air before it's abruptly cut off, just as Emilian sinks his teeth into my skin, the pain blurring my vision. I clench my teeth, swallowing a scream as he pulls deeply, a fire igniting in my chest and spreading throughout my body.

"Emilian," I breathe as nausea rolls through me. "It-it hurts. It fucking *hurts*."

He doesn't pull away, even as my fingers dig into his skin, my body torn between pushing him away and pulling him closer. He's bitten me more times than I can count, and it's never hurt like this. There's always been a moment of pain that was quickly overpowered by ecstasy, but this, this is different. The balance of power is tipping, and I'm the one on the bottom this time. I hear shouts and screams around me, but everything seems so distant, as if there's a bubble surrounding Emilian and me—protecting us from the rest of the world.

Going against every one of my instincts, I push his head into the crook of my neck, his fangs sinking deeper into my flesh, my fingers going numb as agony consumes me. I finally let out a cry as invisible claws sink into my limbs, attempting to pull me down into the bowels of Hell.

"*It will be over soon,*" a voice says. But not just any voice… Emilian's. And it's not coming from his lips that are pressed to my neck, no, it's coming from inside my mind.

"Don't…don't let me go," I croak out, my vision blurring, the edges turning black.

His quiet chuckle flickers through my mind; the claws that were once digging into my skin let go, and the gaping holes they left behind fill with warmth. "*I never intend to,*" he says, but this time his voice is distant, drifting further away. I take in a shuddering breath, but no air enters my lungs, and the world around me fades, pulling me down into the pitch black.

My eyes flutter open; the starless sky above cloaks me in darkness, and the smell of sulfur fills my nostrils. A deafening whistle in my ears muddies my thoughts, a deep ache pulsing through my chest, my body feeling like it's being pricked with a million needles.

I lift myself, bracing on my forearms, as I attempt to blink the blurred edges from my vision. My head throbs, and I groan as I press the heel of my palm against my forehead, squeezing my eyes shut.

"Atlas," a voice says quietly beside me as fingers curl around my bicep. "Say something."

I blink a few times to clear my vision before turning my head to face the person beside me, where I'm met with the familiar red irises. "That fucking hurt," I breathe, and Emilian lets out a quiet sob from where he's holding me. I run my hand down to my chest, pressing into the spot where the symbol is carved. A burning sensation pulses from it, filling me with a fire that seems as though it will never go out. "Am I...?"

Boots pound against the pavement, the smell of embers fills my nose, and Emilian helps me sit up. "Sir Atlas," a deep voice bellows from in front of me. "Are you alright?"

I look up and meet the eyes of my Chancellor, Brander, who stumbles back slightly, his eyes widening with panic. He crouches down, gripping my face in his hand, forcing me to look at him as a growl rumbles from beneath me. His gaze cuts to Emilian. "Did you do this?" he grits out. "Did you—"

"I made the decision myself, Chancellor," I say, pulling my face from his grip. "My life for his."

Rage burns in Brander's eyes as he looks back at me. "This is an act of treason," he growls, looking between us. "If Grand Master Ransley—"

I hear the soft click of boots on the pavement as a voice floats through the alley. "If I what?" the Grand Master says.

Brander pushes to his feet, his hooves clicking against the ground. "Grand Master," he says with a bow, his fist pressing against his heart. "I was just—"

Ransley holds up a hand, silencing him. "I will handle this, Chancellor," he says smoothly. His gaze cuts down to me. "Are you able to stand, Sir Atlas, or do you require assistance?" Without a word, Emilian helps me to my feet, my legs feeling like gelatin as I stumble forward. "Come with me. It seems as though we will be meeting earlier than I expected."

He turns, his eyes sweeping down the alley, taking in the scene of the slaughtered demon, the Legion of wolf shifters, and Jax, who is slumped against the wall, battered and bruised from the fight—a true hero of the Vail. He moves to where Elara stands, her eyes wide with fear as she looks between us, her gaze cutting to the wolf shifters, her body trembling.

"Clean up this mess," Ransley says, not bothering to look at Brander as the command rings out. "I want statements from everyone on what they encountered today and everything leading up to now. I expect a full report by morning."

Brander bows his head, pressing his fist to his chest. "Of course, Grand Master, Sir," he replies, his eyes locking with mine as his brow furrows. Rather than rage, he gazes at me with an expression that I can't quite place before he turns on his hoof and walks away.

Ransley walks past us to the alley entrance, stopping after a few steps to turn and look over his shoulder with a quirked brow. "We don't have long until sunrise," he says matter-of-factly before turning and leading the way out onto the empty street. "And I'm sure you're *starving*, Sir Atlas," he says with a ghost of a smile on his lips.

I look at Emilian, who only stares at Ransley, his expression unreadable. I slip my hand into his, giving it a tight squeeze, feeling the warmth of our palms as they press together. His eyes flick to mine, his brows rising on his forehead. Without a word, we follow Ransley out of the alley and into the wide-open street, leaving any glimmer of doubt that was once between us behind —along with my old life.

21

ATLAS

THE FIRE CRACKLES IN THE HEARTH BEHIND US, WARMING OUR BACKS from where we sit in front of Ransley's desk. His large office inside the cathedral features wall-to-wall, floor-to-ceiling bookshelves filled with books of every size, tightly packed together. He pours himself a goblet of wine, sliding the decanter back to the corner of his desk, the red liquid sloshing against the sides. Delicately, he swirls it before resting the edge on his lips, slowly tilting it back, the liquid flooding his mouth.

The silence is heavy, pressing down on us as he looks between Emilian and me, but the growing hunger inside me weighs even heavier. He lowers the goblet and leans back slightly in his chair, looking down his nose at us. "You've been turned, Sir Atlas," he says, not as an accusation, but a simple fact. "You sacrificed your life to save an illegal vampire." He takes another sip, gazing into the goblet, tilting it as if he's searching for an answer. "And you understand that this act, this *decision*, is treason to the Vail and is punishable by death. Correct?"

I stiffen as I press my own goblet to my mouth, the warm blood he had delivered like sweet nectar on my tongue. Out of the corner of my eye, I see the ghost of a smile on Emilian's lips.

What the fuck is he smiling about?

"It was a decision I made willingly, Grand Master, Sir," I start as I pull the drink from my lips. "It was to save him." I gesture to Emilian. "Who has loyally served as an asset to the Knights of the Vail."

Ransley cocks his head. "And is that all you did it for? There was no other reason to save the being that has been dwelling within your home for the last decade? The same one you have stated on record to have saved yourself?"

I open my mouth to speak, but Emilian leans forward slightly, cutting in. "If anyone is to be punished, Sir—"

Ransley lowers his goblet, the metal ringing as it hits the wooden top of his desk. "No one is being punished," he says with a lethal calmness. "At least, no one that is currently in this room." His gaze cuts to me, and I open my mouth, but the words die on my tongue as Ransley stands up, planting his hands on the desk and leaning forward.

"While it is against the law to feed on a civilian, let alone turn one..." He looks directly at Emilian, "I am willing to turn a blind eye for the good of the Vail. You both seem to have made a decision mutually, which necessarily can't be said for you, can it, Emilian Leblanc?"

I stare at Emilian as the realization hits that I have never bothered to use his last name. He was a human once, and of course, he would have a last name, but I never thought to ask. I was too worried about becoming too close to a monster when I was undoubtedly one myself.

His name is as elegant as he is, and I want to taste it—let it roll around on my tongue and coat the inside of my mouth. It's a delicacy that I want to savor and never share with anyone else.

"No, Sir," Emilian replies, his nails digging into the arm of the chair as he holds Ransley's gaze. "If I'm to be honest, it is a night that haunts me, even after all these years."

Ransley looks at me, his expression still exhaustively unreadable. "And would you say, Sir Atlas, that this night will haunt you, as well? Or will this be a night that you will carry with you —that you will find honor in?"

My mouth gapes, his question throwing me for a loop. I imagined I would be dragged to the dungeons beneath the cathedral, stripped of my rank, and forced to watch as they killed both Emilian and me for such an act. Yet, here we sit, in casual conversation with the Fae who could end our lives at any moment—a simple snap of his fingers and poof, we're erased from existence.

But, no matter what, we would be together in this life and whatever will come after. Now, no one can take that from us.

"It's an honor, Sir," I reply, my throat going dry. It's the only thing I can think to say, as no other words can adequately convey the feeling swirling within me. A mix of hunger and pride gnaws at me, and my chest tightens, "And it's an honor to serve the Vail alongside him."

Ransley quirks a brow, an intrigued look on his face. "And what of your previous partner, Dame Elara? What do you believe should happen to her?"

What Elara did is unforgivable. She not only sought to destroy Emilian but also endangered the city she had once vowed to protect, along with everyone in it. The demon tonight was unlike any I've ever seen, and if that's what's lurking in the deepest parts of Hell, then we'll need stronger forces to hold them off.

"Elara has been my friend since we were children, but what she did tonight—" I start, but someone knocks on the door, and I swallow down the emotion threatening to clog my throat and blink away the stinging in my eyes.

"Come in," Ransley calls, straightening his back as if he's sitting upon a throne.

The door creaks open quietly, and a large, familiar man enters with Elara in tow, her hands clasped behind her back. I immediately recognize him as the man who sat beside us all those evenings ago at the Roundtable. I watch as they pass us, Elara's head bowed, her curls cascading over her forehead, as they go to stand in front of Ransley's desk. Both of them place their fists over their hearts. "Grand Master, Sir," the large man says as he bows his head.

"Sir Vallen," Ransley says, his eyes flicking to Elara, who has yet to look up. "I assume everything at the scene is being taken care of, and any rumors of what happened that might be floating in the inner city have been squashed?"

"Yes, Sir," Vallen says with a curt nod. "My comrades have been instructed to keep quiet about what transpired tonight, and they are aware of the consequences if they fail to do so. Disobeying their Alpha would result in immediate exile."

He's a fucking wolf shifter? That explains why his presence at the Roundtable was so distracting. He possesses more power in one finger than I could have ever imagined in my lifetime, not just as a Knight, but as an Alpha of his pack. He is *not* to be fucked with.

But it begs the question, why does he have Elara? It's not normal protocol for a Knight not to be turned over to their Chancellor, and it's even more rare for the wolves to get involved with anything inside city limits.

I turn and look behind us at the open door, expecting Brander to enter at any moment, but the silence of the hall seeps into the room.

"Very good," Ransley says. I don't miss the sidelong glance that Vallen gives me over his shoulder. A low growl filters through the room, emanating from Emilian as he watches the shifter closely, shifting his weight in his seat, ready to pounce.

"Don't fucking growl at him," I command, the words echoing in the void that has opened inside my mind, drowning out the conversation happening in front of us. *"We're already walking on thin ice, and the last thing we need is for you to challenge a fucking Alpha."*

Emilian stiffens, his head snapping in my direction as if I had screamed it out in the room. I give him a smirk as I look back toward Ransley's desk. *"You've been able to hear my thoughts for quite some time, haven't you? Are you upset that I've figured out your little trick?"*

Emilian gives me a sly smile. *"Have you also figured out that it's something only mates can do?"*

My heart leaps in my chest and my stomach drops, but before I can string another thought together, Ransley's voice rings out, pulling me back. "You will be stripped of your rank and will live among the Silverborne Pack."

"What?" Elara shrieks. "Grand Master, Sir, with all due respect—"

Ransley slams his hands on the top of his desk as he jumps to his feet. *"You* have no respect here," Ransley bites back. "You lost every shred of it when you not only conspired against an asset of the Vail, but your own partner, and endangered the entire city by summoning demons from realms we have worked to keep locked away." His eyes are wild with ire, his glamour slipping slightly to reveal the wicked Fae beneath. "You are lucky that Sir Vallen stepped in and suggested reformation, or else you would not only be stripped of your rank but would be sentenced to death for such acts of treason with immediate execution."

Elara's knees buckle, and on instinct, I jump to my feet, catching her before she hits the floor. I look down at her tear-stained face, her eyes bloodshot and swollen, as the scent of desperation fills my nostrils. It's been years since I've seen her cry; the last time was after an innocent civilian was slaughtered by a rogue Kelpie as it managed to maneuver through the water-lines, drowning people in their own bathtubs.

She stiffens in my hold as she stares back at me, the panic on her face becoming more evident. "Atlas, don't let them do this," she begs, but her words fail to provoke a reaction in me—either I'm still in shock or I just don't fucking care.

"Vampires can allegedly hold grudges for decades for far less than what she has done," Emilian says in my mind. *"For being considered undead, we are quite the emotional beings."*

I don't reply; I just gently lift Elara back upright and step away, her eyes widening further, her pain transforming into fury as she stares into my eyes. "You're...you're a fucking *vampire*," she chokes out as if she's just seeing me for the first time. "He...he *changed* you?"

Emilian shifts but doesn't rise from his seat as he waits for Elara to make one wrong move—overprotective bastard acting as though I can't defend myself. I stay silent as she carries on, each word growing louder. "How could you, Atlas?" she cries out as he points to Emilian. "He lured you in with his allure, and you fucking fell for it. He lured you away from me. *From the Legion*. And you fucking let him." Her eyes are wild as she takes a step toward me, her fury rolling off her. "Do you not understand that I was trying to save you from him? Don't you get that I *love* you? That I've been in love with you for *years*?"

Her breathing is erratic, her eyes wild, as more tears fall down her face, her emotions filling the space between us, making it hard to breathe. "He was slowly draining the life from you, and I had to do something. So, I stole the book from your study, and used it to open rifts, summoning an even stronger demon every time, waiting to watch it rip him to fucking pieces." Her eyes flash to Emilian before flickering back to me. "Don't you see I was trying to help you, Atlas? *Save* you from damnation?"

I'm at a loss for words as I look down at one of the few people who has been by my side for nearly my entire life, and she betrayed me. She was the one who was always in my ear about getting rid of Emilian and that he was as bad, if not worse, than the demons who slipped through from Hell. She saw him as more of a threat than anything we ever fought together, when he was the one who waited patiently for me to get my head out of my ass.

He was always the hero in my story, and he always will be.

I wait for the pain of her betrayal to hit me like a boot to the gut, but nothing comes—not even a glimmer. I think that must have died with me. I shake my head as Emilian rises from his seat and guides me back, his hand pressed against my chest as he steps between Elara and me.

"Allures don't work on *mates*," he bites, the words as sharp as his fangs. "It's why it never has. His decision to discard you was of his own free will." He might as well have slapped her with the stricken look on her face. "He didn't choose you, and he was never going to."

The tension in the room is thick as Vallen sucks in a shallow breath that sounds like a gasp, his eyes widening ever so slightly. Elara's mouth drops open as she stumbles back, bumping into the desk. Ransley looks between us, a satisfied smile plastered on his face. "An admittance of guilt for your records, Sir Vallen," he says in a satisfied tone to match his smile. "Are you sure you want to go through with this?"

Vallen stares at Elara, his eyes as bright as a blood moon, a slight rumble in his chest. "Yes, Grand Master, Sir," he gruffs out, his lip curling up in disgust. "My decision has unfortunately been made."

Ransley's brow quirks as he turns his attention to Elara. "You have one hour to collect your things, and you will be moved to the Silverborne estate *tonight*. Sir Vallen will escort you."

She stutters as she pulls her hands to her chest, clasping them together. "B-but, that's my home. It has been for years." She looks as if she's ready to fall to her knees and beg him for mercy, but still she remains on her feet, a tear escaping and running down her cheek. "I *earned* it."

Ransley lifts his goblet to his lips, taking another long sip, forcing silence between them. "That is housing for tenured Knights," he says coolly, slowly setting his goblet down on his desk with a quiet thunk. "That of which you are no longer."

He looks to Vallen, his eyes darkening. "*One* hour from the time she passes the threshold and not a minute longer." He takes another sip, his eyes flickering toward the door. "You are both dismissed."

Elara releases a sob as Vallen grabs her arm and drags her from the room. He growls as she tries to dig her heels into the floor. "Atlas, please. *I'm sorry.* Don't let them do this. *Please.*" She fights his hold, pushing him away as she whips her head around to me. "Please, I'll do anything to help you forgive me. *Please.*" Vallen effortlessly pulls her through the door and slams it shut, silencing her sobs.

I turn to Ransley, who is watching me intently, waiting for a reaction. "Will she be alright, Grand Master, Sir?" I ask from where I stand, my body going numb even as my chest flickers like a flame.

I don't know how to feel about it all. On one hand, justice has been served to a criminal who received a far lesser sentence than what the law typically allows—someone who was bound and determined to kill my mate. However, on the other hand, she has been my friend since we were children, growing up together in the orphanage and becoming partners. That bond runs so deep that it leaves the waters murky—and maybe that was ultimately our downfall.

I would never have been able to give her what she needs, and hopefully, one day, she'll find it.

Ransley leans back in his chair, steepling his fingers in front of him. "Only time will tell, Sir Atlas," he says with his lips pressed against the edge of his goblet, his gaze shifting between Emilian and me. "Have a seat, we have much to discuss, as I'm sure the question is heavy on your mind about your fate as a Knight of the Vail. Is it not?"

22

ATLAS

STILL CLUTCHING MY GLASS, I BRING IT CLOSER TO MY CHEST AS I swallow the lump in my throat, my back straight as I lower myself into my chair. "And what *is* my fate, Sir?" I ask, looking over my shoulder at Emilian, who is sitting low in his seat, his ankle crossed over his knee, seemingly unbothered.

How can he be so fucking casual at a time like this? Even though the Grand Master has promised to let us live, and after Elara's outburst, I could be stripped of my title, and our heads could still be on the chopping block, or our hearts served skewered on a stake.

"*If you keep comparing us to food, I'll have no choice but to eat you myself*," Emilian says into my mind. My cheeks heat, but instead of replying, I imagine myself flipping him off, unsure if he can see such things in his own head. The answer comes when he huffs out a quiet laugh, one that is buried under the sound of the roaring fire that has made the room near sweltering.

"Fate is written in the stars and whispered to those who are willing to listen," he says, giving me a knowing smile. "And you, Sir Atlas, will continue your duties with your new partner and soon-to-be Knight of the Vail, Emilian Leblanc." His gaze moves slowly to Emilian, and I follow it to see that he's now sitting up straight, his hands curled around the armrest of the chair, wearing a look of surprise on his face.

"With all your active years, there is no need to go through any training. What you don't know, Sir Atlas can fill you in on." He gives me a knowing smile before looking back at Emilian. "I shall schedule your dubbing and make sure that everyone is in attendance for the event—one that I'm sure will go down in history. I will also ensure that there is no question of your loyalty to the Vail, even as you navigate your new state of being, or to your partner, who has proven their loyalty time and time again through their previous lifetime."

"Thank you," Emilian says quietly as he looks at me, his red eyes bright. "It will be an honor to join the Vail and continue to serve...*officially*."

Ransley stands and rounds the desk, extending his hand to Emilian. "You have served well enough already; the rest is simply a formality." Emilian rises to his feet and shakes Ransley's hand, the deep ache in my chest lessening as I look at my new partner in the Vail.

My *mate*.

They both look in my direction as I sit up, feeling a tug in my chest. But this isn't the same tug from my mate; this is something deeper that has been knotted tightly in my chest for almost a lifetime. "Grand Master," I start, and he looks at me almost as if he knows exactly what question is hanging heavy on my tongue. "What do you know about my family? The Delvauxs?"

"I thought you would never ask," he says as he reaches for the decanter and pours himself another glass of wine before rising to his feet and moving to one of the bookshelves behind him. He drags his finger across the spines before stopping and tapping his nail against one. He pulls out a worn, leather-bound book with his free hand. In a huff, he blows off the layer of dust, letting it fall to the floor. He returns to his desk and slowly sits, allowing the book to drop with a dramatic thud.

"And to answer your question, I know much of your family,"

he says, his eyes twinkling. "They were one of the last covens to remain in the city, but ultimately decided to leave just as the wards were being resurrected. All the witches, except for one."

I lean forward like a child being told a bedtime story. "My mother?" I ask softly.

I watch as a ghost of a smile pulls up on his lips. "Your mother, Anya Delvaux, was one of the most powerful witches I had ever seen," he says with a proud gleam in his eyes. "It was fate written in the stars for her to fall in love with a Knight. Your father, Sir Tristan Godwin, was one of the highest ranking in his Legion and was well on his way to becoming a Chancellor."

"Why did the coven leave? And what happened to my parents?" I ask, trying to envision what they both must have looked like with their love-filled gazes.

The pride fades from his eyes, giving way to sorrow. "The covens left to protect their own, as demons were hunting them down and killing them, attempting to destroy their bloodlines and draining their magic dry. Most of the other covens that had resided in Cindervail began to leave nearly a decade earlier, finding solace elsewhere. Still, your mother encouraged hers to stay for as long as possible—to fight and protect their home. It wasn't long after that she met your father and chose to stay permanently, even as the last of her coven, her family, slipped through the wards, leaving the city for good."

Ransley looks down at the book in front of him, flipping it open and turning through the pages. I cock my head to the side as my brows stitch together. "Why, though? Why would she stay behind and risk everything?"

Ransley looks up, his gaze moving between Emilian and me as he lets out a quiet sigh. "*Love*, Sir Atlas. She stayed for love."

I feel a pang in my chest as emotion clogs my throat, attempting to choke me. My fingers grip the armrest, and I feel a warm hand curl brush across my knuckles. I loosen my grip and allow Emilian's fingers to lace through mine, his body leaning toward me from where he is still casually slumped in his chair.

My heart is caught in a vise, squeezing so tightly that the air leaves my lungs.

Is this the feeling that kept my mother here?

"She found out she was pregnant after a year of fighting alongside the Knights in your father's Legion, but they agreed for her to step back and go on light duty until the baby was born. To which, she successfully gave birth to you, Sir Atlas. You were living among a happy family for the first few years of your life in the Delvaux home."

His eyes darken slightly as he takes a shallow breath. "That is, until the night that a horde of demons tore through a rift and ran rampant in your very borough, killing innocents. Your father responded, dying with honor to his name while protecting the city and the family to whom he vowed his life."

My lungs burn, and tears prick at the corners of my eyes. *"Breathe, Atlas,"* Emilian says into my mind, and I let out a shuddered breath. *"You might be a vampire now, but you still have to breathe."*

"And my mother? What happened to her?" I ask, my throat burning.

Ransley's eyes remain filled with sorrow, his voice somber. "She stood at the bottom of the stoop, holding off the same horde that took your father's life until backup forces arrived, and it was then she collapsed from her wounds and took her last breath, but not without telling them you were inside, and arrangements for you had already been made."

Emilian's grip tightens, his thumb caressing my knuckles, doing his best to soothe me. "So, she was prepared to die for me?" I ask, my hands trembling. "She didn't just give me up on a whim?"

Ransley gives me a curt nod as he turns the book around on his desk and slides it toward us. I reach forward to bring it closer and glance at the page written in my mother's handwriting, detailing everything in case something were to happen to her and my father. I flip through several pages until the words run out, leaving me with only blank parchment. Flipping back, I see that at the bottom of the page are both of my parents' signatures in red ink.

No, not ink...*blood*.

Ransley nods to the book in my hand. "They loved you more than anything, Sir Atlas, including themselves. They had everything prepared to ensure that you lived the life you were destined to and that you were cared for properly. I oversaw that every detail of your parents' wishes was met and, oftentimes, exceeded. I had the letter sent to the Headmaster on your eighteenth birthday, and I watched from the shadows as he showed you back to your family's home."

I stare at their blood-marked signatures, running my finger along the edge of the page, careful not to touch them, as Ransley continues. "They would both be very proud of who you've become, Sir Atlas," he says, a slight rasp in his voice. "They were powerful beings who used it for the greater good of Cindervail. And it's obvious you walk the same path, especially now, as you've found something else that's worth fighting for. Something that many will go their entire lives searching for."

I look up at him, but I notice that he's focused on Emilian, who rests his fist over his chest as his gaze turns to me. "It will be an honor to serve the city under the Delvaux name, as it was their home that I was invited into and their bloodline that has kept me safe and well fed for the last decade." He lifts the hand, still linked with mine, to his lips, pressing them gently against my skin before letting his teeth scrape across my knuckle. "And I will do everything in my power to thank them tenfold for all they have done by bringing my mate into the world...and into my afterlife."

The worlds I tried so hard to keep apart collide, and the feelings I buried deep inside myself bubble to the surface just as the clock strikes five o'clock in the morning, leaving us with only an hour until sunrise—finally bringing an end to this feverishly long night.

Ransley rises to his feet and rounds the desk, gesturing toward the door. "I'll have your newest mission sent to you in four days. That should give you time to rest adequately and more time to adjust to your new way of life." Ransley places his fist over his heart, the slightest of smiles still on his face as he says, "Rise for the Vail."

Emilian nods, mirroring my actions as I bow and place my fist over my heart. "Where evil will fall," we reply in unison before turning to leave.

I lead us out into the night, but instead of slinking into the shadows, we walk side by side down the middle of the street until we reach an alley, where he suddenly pulls me into the darkness.

"Emilian," I say breathlessly, "What are you doing?"

The bricks are rough against my back as he presses against me, his sharp mouth hovering, our breaths mingling. "Hopefully you," he says as his mouth presses against mine, unleashing our monsters as we let our desires for one another take over, our claws and teeth battling it out—finally winning this ten-year war.

EPILOGUE

ONE MONTH LATER

EMILIAN

"Emilian." My name is no more than a whisper as I drag my tongue up the column of Atlas's throat, the taste of him making me even harder, my cock twitching. I curl around him, pressing my length against his ass so he can feel exactly what it does to me when he has my name on his lips.

What he's always done to me.

The only thing between us is his boxers, which I'm not afraid to tear away at a moment's notice.

"How long am I supposed to wear this fucking thing?" he asks as my hand comes around his throat, looping my finger through the O-ring of the very collar that was removed from me the night he turned—no longer the house pet, but an equal.

Mates.

"Possibly as long as you made me wear it," I say roughly as I drag him back, gliding my free hand down his side and smacking his ass with a pop. "Maybe even longer now that we have eternity to play," I tease, nipping at his ear and gently kissing down his neck.

He groans as I sink my teeth into the crook of his neck, drawing out his sweet blood, the flavor only slightly altered since I changed him—his essence mixed with mine. I grind into his backside, letting my other hand slide under the waistband of his boxers, gripping his thick, hard cock.

The last month has been the best of my mortal and immortal lives combined. Atlas has been giving in to his desires, and I've been enjoying the benefits as he takes the time to explore more about himself, discovering the parts that he kept hidden from the world. His immortal body recovers quickly from our exertions, and while we've already been on numerous missions and should be on the brink of exhaustion, we can't seem to keep our hands off each other.

Even in his undead life, he's more alive than ever before.

The morning we returned home from the Grand Master's office, he immediately moved my things from the basement to the bedroom next to his—which I have yet to sleep in since he insists I sleep in his bed every day. It was as nice a gesture as him being on his knees before me, sucking me off as he begged for forgiveness for being what he refers to as a "fucking jackass" for the last decade.

I must say, I love how he grovels at my feet, begging for me, and taking me as if he were made for me, just as I seem to have been made for him.

Our bond as mates has only grown stronger, letting me feel his every emotion, just as he can feel mine. This connection works wonders out in the field, and I'm sure that once the honeymoon period wears off, maybe in a few decades, we'll be able to tame the emotions and put back up a mental wall. But for now, I love feeling how raw he is, those feelings coursing through me, keeping me attuned to his desires and helping me assess his needs—something I so desperately wished I had when I was adjusting to my own change.

When we arrived at the first Roundtable after that fateful night, I was prepared to be dragged out with a stake through my heart for baring my teeth if someone merely looked at Atlas the wrong way. Instead, his friends who remained in the Knighthood greeted him as they normally would. A few were kind enough to ask how he was feeling, while others approached me with caution but without the same disdain as before.

The Basilisk, Jax, not only acknowledged me, but he even took the time to shake my hand and congratulate me on officially becoming a Knight of the Vail. Amidst all the chaos, I caught the Grand Master's gaze, receiving an approving nod, while sharing a knowing look as his eyes flickered between Atlas and me, just as Atlas took a long draw from the blood flask in his pocket, suppressing his hunger while in public.

Atlas comes from a long line of blood witches, which I confirmed after looking further into the grimoire his previous partner had stolen. This more than explains how he is already in such control of himself. Even though he has no abilities—since he was born male and no one was around to teach him how to harbor any ounce of magic he could have possibly manifested— he remains powerful in his own right. His bloodline gives him as much power in this city as any magic would.

"*Emilian*," he groans again, pulling me from my thoughts, as his hips buck from where my hand glides along his cock. "If you don't stop, I'm going to come in your hand," he grits out, reaching between us to roughly grip my length. "Fuck me, *now*."

I chuckle, the sound as dark as the stormy, moonless night that covers the city. I pull back on the collar, sinking my teeth into the crook of his neck again. "Beg for me, *pet*," I say from the corner of my mouth, his blood escaping and running down my chin. "I want to hear how much you *want* me. How much you *need* me."

He tries to shift, but I hold him tightly against me as I swirl my tongue over the punctures on his neck. "Emilian, if you don't fuck me, I'll—" he gasps out.

I tighten my hold, taking a bite from his shoulder this time, the feel of his skin giving way under my fangs making me harder as I sense him coming undone from beneath me. I grip his boxers and shred them into ribbons with my claws. "You'll what?" I croon as I press my cock against him. "Muzzle me?" He gasps as I push into him, my own precum coating me, helping me slide into him with ease.

I can't help but let out a dark chuckle as he lets loose a guttural moan. I roll us, pushing him face down into the mattress and filling his ass to my hilt. "Fuck, Atlas, you feel so fucking good," I say between thrusts, my balls already tightening as a tingle runs up my spine. "I am going to fill you with my cum, and if you're a good boy, I just might let *you* come tonight, too."

He moans into the sheets, my claws pricking his skin. His blood wells around my fingertips, turning them crimson, as the intoxicating smell of him hits my senses and wracks through me.

A roar fills the room, vibrating against the windows as I come, my body shuddering from my sudden orgasm. I reach down, grip his brown hair, and pull his head up from the mattress, forcing his flushed face to look over his shoulder at me.

"Is that all you've got?" he teases breathlessly, his eyes wild with desire.

I grin wildly, my fangs elongating. I love it when he tries to flip the script, thinking he can take control, but it only happens when I let him. He might be next in line for a Chancellor position, but he knows full well that he's not the one in charge when we're in this house—in this bed.

I pull out and flip him over, his mussed hair falling over his forehead as his precum drips down his cock, pooling onto his abs. I climb over him and pin his wrists to the bed. "I'm going to tie you up and fuck you all over again, and then we'll see if I'll let you come. How's that sound, my little white knight?"

His eyes flash with a hunger that's deeper than the one he has for blood, his deep red irises burning bright. "You really are a fucking monster," he says with a breathless smile.

"But I'm *your* monster," I say as I press a kiss to his lips.

"And now I'm yours?" he asks with a gleam in his eyes that toes the line of pride.

"You were mine long before now," I say, leaning down and

burrowing my face in the crook of his neck, swirling my tongue over the blood that still trickles down from one of the many bites I've left behind that now decorate his body. "And mine you'll forever be."

I pull the leather straps out from the headboard and buckle them around his wrists. It was the perfect addition to the bed; one I was wholly surprised he agreed to install. Atlas has always needed to be tied to the bed and fucked to the edge of his immortal life, and now I get to do it whenever I want.

I slant my mouth over his, drawing him into a deep kiss, letting him taste his sweet blood that still coats my tongue. I pull away, dragging my teeth over his lip, and letting it loose with a pop. I nip his skin as I work back down his body, making sure to swirl my tongue over every spot. His hisses and moans of pleasure are a symphony of ecstasy that would send me to the heavens above if I weren't already damned for all eternity.

I hover over his length, the smell of his desire making my mouth water as I take in the mess he's already made of himself. "So, you *do* want me," I say with a chuckle before gliding my tongue up and over the head of his throbbing cock, keeping my eyes locked on him, watching him become nothing more than putty in my hands. "So fucking delicious. A meal I will never tire of."

I grip him and slowly pump my hand up and down his length, teasing him as I drag my tongue through his slit. His hips shift as I push back one of his legs, sinking my teeth into the flesh of his inner thigh.

"Oh *fuck*," he gasps, his back arching off the bed. "Emilian, I'm…I'm going to come," he pants, the leather straps groaning as his body bucks beneath my hold.

"*Come for me*," I say into his mind as I take a long pull of his blood. I speed up the motion of my hand until his hips slam up, and I watch as streams of cum explode across his abs, his sounds of pleasure enough to turn me into a feral beast.

I wipe my hand across the mess of his desire that shines

across his skin and coat my own needy cock. Pushing his legs back, I don't hesitate as I slam into him, both of us moaning as I fuck him harder than before.

"When we arrive at the meeting tonight," I say with a growl between thrusts. "I want every man, woman, and monster to know just who you fucking belong to." A tingle rushes up my spine, and my head falls back as another roar erupts from me, once again filling him to the brim with my seed. "What's *mine*."

He's flushed, a delicious sheen of his blood, sweat, and cum coating him. I can't help but run my hands through it and lick them clean, groaning as each finger pops from my lips. I could admire him like this for the rest of time, tied up and filthy, until the devil himself drags us to Hell.

He chuckles, looking down at himself. "I think they already know, Emilian." He gives me a smirk. "Jax has already made a comment or two about it."

My lips quirk up, slowly pulling back into a grin, showing off my blood-coated fangs. "And *what* exactly is your little reptilian friend saying?" I ask, lowering my head and pressing a kiss to his pelvic bone, and I can't help but notice that he seems to be ready for another round—a feral little fledgling.

He sighs heavily as his head falls back on the pillow, his cock twitching as it lengthens further—for such a strong being, he's far too easy to control with a simple kiss.

He chuckles as he gently pulls on his restraints. "Just that the mix of blood and cum is my new signature scent, and I'll never have to worry about being hit on again. Not that I was being hit on much before, but that's beside the point."

I give him another kiss as I gently run my claws down his inner thigh. "You know, that night that you fucked that woman," I say lowly, his head lifting to meet my gaze, his eyes widening. "I nearly broke through the bars of my enclosure at the thought of someone else's hands on you. I would have killed her for touching what was mine—drank her dry and made her disappear for good, finally getting to keep you all to myself."

Atlas chuckles, but the sound is dry, an acknowledgement of my truth. "No one has ever had me like you do, Emilian," he says quietly. "All the years I fought you off, denying what I felt about you, and locked you away, are years I intend to make up. It was always going to be you...But I was too afraid of what that meant. And when I nearly lost you, I knew I had to admit the truth, not only to myself, but to you, too."

"And what truth is that?" I ask, cocking my head to the side.

He scrapes his fangs over his bottom lip hard enough to draw blood, the smell filling my nose as I continue to kiss across his inner thigh, listening to his sweet confession. "That I love you, Emilian."

My head snaps up at his words, my gaze getting lost in his. "Do you know how long I've waited to hear those words tumble from your lips?" I ask, my mouth going dry. "And how long I've waited to say them with mine?"

"Say them now," he breathes. I watch as the prominence of his throat bobs, the scent of his anxiety swirling in the air. "Tell me. *Please.*"

"You are my knight in shining armor, Atlas, and I have loved you from the moment I laid eyes on you, sprawled out beneath that demon on that blood-soaked street. I knew you were meant to be mine by the way you refused to die, willing to fight off the demon until you were to take your last breath." I press my fingers into his skin, ensuring he's still real. "You are my light in the darkness, my mate, and the love I have so desperately wanted. No, that I've *needed.*"

We're both frozen, suspended in time as he smiles softly at me, looking more handsome than I've ever seen him. "Next time," he starts, "I'm tying *you* to the bed and having you confess your love for me all over again, *sire,*" he teases, saying the last word with a gentle scoff.

I give him a sly smile just as the grandfather clock chimes through the house, allowing us only an hour before we're due to meet for the Roundtable. "But I love seeing you at my mercy and hearing you beg," I growl as the final chime resonates throughout the house.

I relish the sound of my name as it slips from his lips while I suck him dry, reminding everyone in the Vail who he *truly* vowed his life to—the same one he loves, who would not only kill for him but also die again for him, and whom he would find waiting in the next life, ready to do it all over.

As Knights, we both Rise for the Vail.

Where evil will fall.

About the Author

KL Hill has always been a maladaptive daydreamer with a boundless imagination, often lost in the wild stories she creates. She lives in Indiana with her husband, their dogs and cats, chickens, and racing pigeons.

If you enjoy her work, visit **www.klhillauthor.com** to subscribe to her Substack for weekly updates, serial chapters, and exclusive content.